Philip Ridley was born in the East End of London, where he still lives and works. He studied painting at St Martin's School of Art and by the time he graduated had exhibited widely throughout Europe and written his first book. As well as three books for adults, and the highly acclaimed screenplay for *The Krays* feature film, he has written three successful stage plays: *The Pitchfork Disney*, *The Fastest Clock in the Universe* and *Ghost from a Perfect Place*. He has also written and directed two films: *The Reflecting Skin* – winner of eleven international awards – and *The Passion of Darkly Noon*. Philip Ridley has written seven other books for children: *Mercedes Ice*, *Dakota of the White Flats*, *Krindlekrax* (winner of the Smarties Prize and the W. H. Smith Mind-Boggling Books Award), *Meteorite Spoon*, *Kasper in The Glitter*, *Dreamboat Zing* and *The Hooligan's Shampoo*. *Kasper in The Glitter* was nominated for the 1995 Whitbread Children's Book Award.

Chris Riddell lives in Brighton. He studied art at the Epsom School of Art and Design and Brighton Polytechnic. He has illustrated a wide range of children's books, including *Mercedes Ice*, *Dakota of the White Flats*, *Meteorite Spoon*, *Kasper in The Glitter* and *Dreamboat Zing*, and two picture books: *Something Else* by Kathryn Cave (shortlisted for the Smarties Prize and the Kate Greenaway Award) and Alan Durant's *Angus Rides the Goods Train*. He is also the political cartoonist for the *Observer*.

Other books by Philip Ridley

DAKOTA OF THE WHITE FLATS
KASPER IN THE GLITTER
KRINDLEKRAX
MERCEDES ICE
METEORITE SPOON
ZINDERZUNDER

Philip Ridley

Scribbleboy

Illustrated by Chris Riddell

PUFFIN BOOKS

PUFFIN BOOKS

Published by the Penguin Group
Penguin Books Ltd, 27 Wrights Lane, London W8 5TZ, England
Penguin Books USA Inc., 375 Hudson Street, New York, New York 10014, USA
Penguin Books Australia Ltd, Ringwood, Victoria, Australia
Penguin Books Canada Ltd, 10 Alcorn Avenue, Toronto, Ontario, Canada M4V 3B2
Penguin Books (NZ) Ltd, 182–190 Wairau Road, Auckland 10, New Zealand

Penguin Books Ltd, Registered Offices: Harmondsworth, Middlesex, England

First published by Viking 1997
Published in Puffin Books 1997
7 9 10 8

Filmset in Stone Serif

Made and printed in England by Clays Ltd, St Ives plc

British Library Cataloguing in Publication Data
A CIP catalogue record for this book is available from the British Library

ISBN 0–140–36894–9

For Kelsey –
may you always be true to your scribbles

MONDAY

— 1 —

Scribbletation**s**, New Kid

Welcome to the neighbourhood!

Don't know your name yet (that'**s** why I've addre**ss**ed the envelope to 'The New Kid Around Here') . . . but let me introduce my**s**elf.

My name i**s** Ziggy Fuzz.

I'm the Pre**s**ident of a very **s**pecial fan club.

And I'd like you – ye**s**, you, New Kid Around Here! – to join.

The full title of the fan club i**s** the **S**cribbleboy Fan Club.

Now, a**s** you're a New Kid Around Here, you're probably wondering who **S**cribbleboy i**s**.

So let me explain!

If you look around the neighbourhood, you'll *s*ee lot*s* of graffiti. Mo*s*t of it i*s* totally ugly and boring. But there are *s*ome piece*s* of graffiti that are not totally ugly and boring at all. That'*s* becau*s*e . . . they're not graffiti!

They're *s*cribble*s*!

*s*cribble*s* *s*cribbled by the mo*s*t *s*cribbledaciou*s* and *s*cribblefabulou*s* *s*cribbler in *s*cribbledom.

Hi*s* name?

*s*CRIBBLEBOY!!!

You're very lucky, New Kid Around Here, becau*s*e there happen*s* to be a *s*cribble very clo*s*e to you. If you want to *s*ee it (and I'm *s*ure after reading thi*s* you'll be ru*s*hing to get an eyeful), then leave your flat*s*, cro*ss* the *s*quare, and walk down the concrete path until you reach the playground.

At the back of thi*s* playground i*s* . . .

A *s*CRIBBLE!

Before you go, though, a word of warning: don't mention *s*cribbleboy to grown-up*s*! I've noticed you live with your dad and older brother – and I'm *s*ure they're very nice – but, a*s* grown-up*s*, they will not be capable of appreciating the full *s*cribblewonderment of *s*cribbleboy.

If, when you *s*ee the *s*cribble, it *s*wirl*s* and whirl*s* in*s*ide you (like it *s*wirl*s* and whirl*s* in*s*ide me), then . . .

JOIN THE *s*CRIBBLEBOY FAN CLUB!!!

There are hundred*s* of u*s*!

If not thou*s*and*s*!

We meet every Tue*s*day afternoon at 5.30

in the old cinema down the Big Road (just walk to the back of your flats and turn left into the Big Road – the old cinema is on the right).

I look forward to seeing you there, New Kid Around Here.

Scribbleboy For Ever

Ziggy Fuzz

President of the Scribbleboy Fan Club

PS If this letter is opened by mistake – either by the New Kid Around Here's dad or the New Kid Around Here's brother – then it shouldn't have been, as I clearly marked the envelope, 'TO THE NEW KID AROUND HERE. VERY PRIVATE AND PERSONAL. NOT TO BE OPENED BY ANY GROWN-UPS!'

PPS The letter 'S' on my typewriter don't work!

'What are you reading, kiddo?'

'Oh . . . n-nothing, Mont.'

'So why are you hiding it?'

'I'm n-not!'

'You are!'

'It's just j-junk mail, Mont. That's all.'

'If you say so, kiddo. Budge up!' He squeezed next to Bailey. 'Let me ask you something else! Why are you sitting out here? It's the most unwhizzeroonie place I can think of.'

They were on the concrete steps in their block of flats: a cold, damp place, covered with graffiti. The only light came from a flickering – and ominously crackling – neon strip above.

'The Skipper's h-hoovering the flat again,' Bailey explained. 'I've c-come out here to do some r-reading.' He tapped a rolled-up comic in his jacket pocket.

Bailey Silk was eleven years old, had a round face,

blue eyes, crewcut hair and – what many grown-ups described as – 'serious eyes'. He was wearing his school uniform: dove-grey blazer, white shirt, black and white striped tie, charcoal-grey trousers and black shoes. It was uncomfortable at the best of times, but during the summer – which it now was – became almost unbearable.

Monty, his brother, was in a uniform too. Though, being nineteen years old, it had nothing to do with school. He'd just got a job in Pizza Most Yum-Yum, a local restaurant, and all the employees had to wear a green cap, green shoes, green socks, green and white striped shirt (short-sleeved) and green trousers.

Like Bailey, Monty had a round face, blue eyes and crewcut hair. Unlike his brother, he had the most unworried face imaginable, with wide, sparkling eyes and – what most people described as – 'an infectious grin'.

'You're not reading, kiddo,' Monty said, nudging Bailey. 'You're brooding! Look how deep your frown is.' He rubbed his thumb between his brother's eyebrows.

'I'm n-not frowning!' snapped Bailey.

'All right, kiddo, all right,' soothed Monty, realizing he'd touched a sore point. 'Only teasing.' He gave Bailey a hug, then jumped to his feet. 'Don't stay out here too long! That flashing light'll make your eyes bad.' He started bounding up the steps two at a time. 'And don't forget dinner's at seven, kiddo! The Skipper'll go whacko if you're late.'

Bailey waited for Monty's footsteps to disappear, then reread the letter.

Scribbleboy! he thought. Scribbles! Scribbledacious! Scribblefabulous!

The words were like a magic spell.

Enticing him . . .

To the Scribble!

So what did Bailey's new neighbourhood – or 'Around Here' as the letter called it – look like?

Well, in a word, grey.

Grey concrete buildings, grey concrete walls and grey concrete pathways. Most of the concrete was covered in a mixture of graffiti, birds' mess and weeds. Where some of the concrete had cracked, or fallen away altogether, it had been replaced with corrugated iron.

That's *grey* corrugated iron, of course.

At least my uniform blends in! thought Bailey. Like camouflage. When soldiers go into the jungle they wear green to merge with the trees and grass. So here – it's grey! Ah! Here's the playground!

To be honest, it wasn't much of a playground: a broken seesaw, a single swing, a sandpit without any sand (old tin cans had long since taken its place) and a metal staircase that had once led to a slide, but now led nowhere.

Like a ghost-town! thought Bailey.

And then . . .

He saw it!

On the concrete wall.

He gasped.

For the concrete wall was covered with the brightest, most eye-scorching colours Bailey had ever seen.

So many colours that no sign of concrete remained. Just . . .

Emerald green! Ruby red! Sapphire blue!

All whirling and wheeling together!

A kaleidoscope of stars, circles, crescent moons, comets!

Everything twirling and twisting!

Churning and whirling!
Swirling!
'SCRIBBLEBOY!' Bailey cried out.
Then he fainted ...

— 4 —

'Sweetheart?'

Bailey opened his eyes.

A young woman was staring down at him: bright red lips, bright pink hair (dyed, of course, and tied in a ponytail on top of her head) and the longest, thickest false eyelashes Bailey had ever seen.

I've never fainted before! Bailey thought. What a strange feeling! Like disappearing for a while.

He got to his feet, still feeling a little wobbly.

'Careful, sweetheart!' the young woman warned him. 'Perhaps you should go to the hospital – any bumps, cuts or grazes? Let me see, no, look into my eyes, sweetheart, well, your eyes are just peachy-dandy, no damage done by the look of things.'

She spoke so fast Bailey could barely keep up with her. He just gazed, nodding and shaking his head whenever he thought fit.

'You gave me quite a scare, sweetheart, lying there on the ground, lucky I was passing, don't usually come this way, but there were some roadworks at the traffic lights, so I made a little detour, and what do I see? A boy – you, sweetheart! – lying on the ground, and my heart missed a beat, or jumped into my mouth –

whatever the saying is – and I rushed over and said, "Sweetheart," and it must have been the magic word because your eyes opened and my heart stopped missing a beat, and slid back down my throat – whatever the saying is – and now here we are, all peachy-dandy, and I've got to ask, because I'm a nosy kind of article, what happened, sweetheart, did you fall off the swing?'

'Er . . . affirmative.'

'Affirma-what, sweetheart?'

'Affirm – oh, I mean y-y-yes.'

Bailey could feel the Scribble behind him, throbbing and pulsating like an animal waiting to pounce. He wanted to turn and look at it. But –

Don't! he thought. The last thing I want is to get dizzy again.

'Can you walk, sweetheart?'

'Er . . . affirma – I mean, y-y-yes.'

'I know what affirmative means now, sweetheart, I'm not as silly as I look, "affirmative" means yes, so you must say "negative" for no, am I right, sweetheart?'

Bailey nodded.

'And stop looking so serious, sweetheart,' she giggled. 'That's the deepest frown I've ever seen.'

— 9 —

'I'm not f-frowning,' said Bailey irritably. 'It's w-what I look like. I was b-born serious.'

'Well, I'm just the person to put an end to your natural-born seriousness, sweetheart.'

'H-how?'

'The Ice-Cream Diagnosis!'

'The w-what?'

She grinned. 'Follow me.'

— 5 —

On the other side of the road was an ice-cream van.

'That's the Spanglemobile, sweetheart!'

The van was covered with paintings of ice-creams and ice-lollies and there were fairy lights (like the ones you put on your Christmas tree) round all the windows. Across the side of the van, in neon colours, was written, 'DOCTOR SPANGLE'S SPANGFABULOUS ICE-CREAMS.'

'Doctor Sp-Spangle?' asked Bailey.

'That's me, sweetheart, should have introduced myself earlier, Tiffany Spangle, the Ice-Cream Doctor, and there's not a frown in the world that can't be smoothed away by one of my specially prepared remedies ...' Tiffany opened the van door and led Bailey inside. 'Welcome to my surgery, sweetheart!'

Boxes and jars were everywhere. Each one full of chocolate buttons, or raisins, or coconut flakes, or hundreds and thousands, or wafers, or chocolate flakes, or glacé cherries. There was a large freezer full of lollies and choc-ices and, beside the serving hatch, a silver ice-cream machine. It made a gentle, electric purring noise that Bailey found somehow comforting.

'Sit down, sweetheart, on that box will be fine, that's perfect . . . now, first your pulse.'

'My w-what?'

'That throbbing thing in your wrist, let me feel.'

'W-why?'

'I told you, sweetheart, I've got to make my diagnosis, just like any doctor, only a doctor of medicine will give you medicine, whereas I – being a Doctor of Ice-Cream – will give you –'

'Ice-Cream!'

'Affirmative, sweetheart, what a brainbox you are, and – as you see – I'm using your "affirmative" word already, so I must be a brainbox too – now, pulse please!'

Bailey gave her his hand.

'Mmmm, you need chocolate ice-cream to start with, that's for sure . . . chocolate and *orange* to be precise!'

Bailey gasped. 'Affirmative, Tiffany! That's my f-favourite!'

'Of course it is, sweetheart, I never make mistakes where ice-cream is concerned . . . Now your temperature!' She laid her hand on Bailey's forehead. 'Mmmm – yes! – coconut flakes!'

'Right again, Tiffany!' cried Bailey, grinning with excitement.

'Tongue, sweetheart.'

'W-what?'

'That thing in your mouth that wiggles when you talk, not that you're talking much, but, then again, I'm talking enough for both of us, and don't be bashful, sweetheart, I've seen more tongues than you've had hot dinners, or should I say, more tongues than your *tongue*'s had hot dinners.'

Bailey poked his tongue out.

Tiffany pinched it between her thumb and forefinger. 'Mmmm, you need two chocolate flakes . . .'

Bailey nodded enthusiastically.

' . . . and almond nuts.'

More nodding.

'Oh, I'm going to make you a special to end all specials,' said Tiffany, letting go of his tongue, 'and I'm going to call it a Spangle Special à la – oh, what's your name, sweetheart?'

'Bailey.'

'A Spangle Special à la Bailey! How does that sound, sweetheart?'

'Ultra-delicious, Tiffany!' Bailey licked his lips with anticipation.

Tiffany got a cone and proceeded to make the Special.

Look at Tiffany's ponytail! thought Bailey. She's rolling her head round so fast, it's spinning like a propeller! She'll take off in a minute!

Tiffany caught his look. 'Don't worry about my hair, sweetheart,' she said. 'It always spins like this when I get excited. Now I'll just sprinkle some hundreds and

thousands on top to finish, everyone likes them –
aaannnd – *voilà*! A Spangle Special à la Bailey!' She
handed it to Bailey. 'Lick away, sweetheart!'

Carefully, Bailey licked. 'Mega-ultra-delicious,
Tiffany!' he cried. His eyes grew wide with sweet
delight.

'I knew you'd like it, sweetheart, and look – I do
believe your frown has faded just a little. Doctor
Spangle strikes again!' She watched Bailey eat for a
while, then asked, 'You must be new around here,
sweetheart?'

'Mmmm . . . affirmative.'

'And where do you live, sweetheart?'

'In the b-big block of flats.'

'Not the ones at the end of the path?'

'Mmmm . . . '

'Well, what a small world, sweetheart, I live in the
same block of flats. With my grandfather – Wait a
minute! You haven't got a brother, have you,
sweetheart?'

'Mmmm.'

'Who works in Pizza Most Yum-Yum?'

'Mmmm.'

'Oh, I've seen him around, sweetheart. He's got the
cutest little grin I've ever seen –'

'I've g-got to go now,' Bailey said suddenly, getting to
his feet.

'What's wrong, sweetheart? Have I said something
wrong?'

'Negative! It's j-just that . . . well, dinner's in a f-few
minutes!'

'I'll drive you, sweetheart –'

'Q-quicker to run!' Bailey finished his ice-cream and
opened the van door. 'And by the w-way, my brother's
not *really* grinning. His mouth's j-just grin-shaped. Bye!'

— 6 —

'You're almost late, Trooper Two!' declared the
Skipper.

'S-sorry, Skipper,' said Bailey, sitting at the kitchen
table. He glanced at Monty, who was sitting opposite.

Monty winked.

Bailey smiled and winked back.

'And look at you, Trooper Two,' the Skipper
continued, oblivious to the fact that his children

weren't really taking him *that* seriously, 'panting like a hippopotamus –'

'Oh, don't carry on, Skip,' interrupted Monty.

'Oh ... er ... affirmative, Trooper One,' said the Skipper, and looked bashfully at his plate.

'Besides,' continued Monty, 'I bet I know what the kiddo's been up to. Exploring the new neighbourbood. Right, kiddo?'

'Affirmative, Mont!'

'You see, Skip! He's been doing some ... oh, what's the word, Skip? When a trooper takes a look around a new place?'

'Reconnaissance!' announced the Skipper.

'That's the word: reconnaissance! You know everything, Skip.'

Monty can wrap the Skipper round his little finger! thought Bailey. What would I do without him – oh, well, best start eating. Oh, surprise, surprise! Fishfingers and chips!

This is what the Skipper always cooked for dinner. He'd once seen a movie about the army, you see, where a general declared, 'Fishfingers and chips is the perfect meal for the military man!'

In fact, the Skipper – or Mr Silk to give him his civilian name – got most of what he said, did and wore from watching films about the army, navy or airforce. His clothes, for example, were not only from different armed forces, but from different periods in history: an eighteenth-century admiral's hat with a fluffy white feather (as seen in a film called *Mutiny on the Bounty*), a white jacket (as seen in *An Officer and a Gentleman* – the Skipper's second favourite film, by the way), khaki shorts (as seen in a film about desert warfare) and knee-high boots, a monocle and a moustache (as seen in a film about the First World War).

'Time to stop eating, Troopers.' The Skipper jumped to his feet and started to wash up the dishes. They didn't have any dessert, as the Skipper had 'never seen any soldier or sailor or pilot eating rhubarb crumble and custard'.

'Now, Skip, tell me something,' said Monty, as casually as he could. 'Why didn't you go to the Unemployment Office and sign on today?'

Bailey could see the Skipper tense.

'I intended to go, Trooper One,' mumbled the Skipper, twiddling his moustache, 'but ... the flat needed hoovering.'

'You'll have to go tomorrow, Skip. My wages ain't enough to keep us. We need more money. Just look at the state of HQ.'

Their new flat was clean and tidy (after all, that's what the Skipper did: the housework, endlessly), but there were no carpets, and all the furniture was years old and faulty in some way. The sofa, for example, had had half its stuffing pulled out by Bailey (he had been only a baby at the time, I hasten to add), the beds were too uncomfortable for words (Monty's even had a spring sticking up through its mattress), and the fridge had a tendency to defrost and flood the kitchen whenever it took the fancy.

'Well, I've got to skedaddle,' declared Monty, suddenly getting to his feet. 'I'm doing an extra shift tonight. Bye, Skip. Bye, kiddo.' And, before they'd had a chance to say 'Bye' back, he'd dashed out.

Bailey looked at his dad.

Poor Skipper, he thought. He's dreading going to the Unemployment Office.

'I'll tell you w-what, Skipper,' said Bailey. 'Why don't I go with you t-t-tomorrow. K-keep you company.'

'Very kind of you, Trooper Two,' said the Skipper.

'Moral support always welcome!' He emptied the dishwater. 'Now it's time to keep watch.'

The Skipper went into the hallway and sat on the wooden chair next to the phone. He stared at the phone intently, waiting for it to ring.

Bailey made his way to his bedroom. 'She's going to r-ring very soon, Skipper,' he said. 'I j-just know it!'

'I hope so, Trooper Two,' sighed the Skipper, polishing his monocle. 'I certainly miss my other half.' He sighed deeply. 'It's been sixty-four days, ten hours and twenty-two minutes.'

Bailey went to his bedroom and sat on the edge of his mattress.

Sixty-four days, ten hours, twenty-two – now twenty-three – minutes, he thought. That's how long it's been since ... Mum left.

— 7 —

Don't think about it, thought Bailey. I'll only end up crying. And what's the point of that? Oh, why can't I just cut off my thoughts? After all, when you don't want to see: you close your eyes. When you don't want to smell: you pinch your nose. When you don't want to hear: you stick cotton wool in your ears. So why can't you stop thinking about things? Because I don't want to think about her! I don't! I don't!

But, instinctively, his hand was reaching for the letter.

About two months ago he'd found it on the pillow when he woke up one morning. It was the first letter Bailey had ever received, and the last one he ever wanted.

Dearest Cherub –

By the time you wake up I will be gone.

It's difficult for me to explain why I had to leave. You're too young to understand. But, one day, you will be old enough to realize that I'm doing the right thing.

I've got to have some time alone to think.

When I've thought enough, I'll phone. Until that day, you and Monty must look after Dad.

Love,

Mum

XXX

She left me! thought Bailey, suddenly angry.

His moods could change so quickly when he thought of his mum. One minute he was sad and wanted her back more than anything, the next he was angry and never wanted to see her again.

I don't care if she *never* comes back! Good riddance! She couldn't have loved me very much in the first place! Not to just get up and go like that! And if she doesn't love me, then there's no point in me missing her.

And then –

He saw all the piles of super hero comics beside his

— 18 —

bed. And he remembered: his mum had bought them for him. Every one of them. Every Saturday morning she'd come back from the market and say, 'Guess what Mummy's got for her little cherub?' And she'd take two, sometimes even three comics from her shopping bag. 'That's for being such a cherub for Mummy,' she'd say, her voice as gentle as feathers falling on snow.

Think of something else! he thought. But what?

And then it hit him!

Scribbleboy!

He lay back on the bed and imagined the Scribble in the playground.

Immediately, he felt things whirling and swirling inside him.

He was back in that world of emerald green, ruby red, sapphire blue . . .

— 8 —

'Kiddo?'

Bailey's eyes clicked open.

Monty was standing at the foot of the bed, grinning. 'Nodded off, eh?' His grin got wider. 'Bet it was a whizzeroonie dream. You were smiling like you didn't have a care in the world. Now, you best get undressed and hop into bed. It's very late – oh, before I forget! Here's your magazine.' He handed Bailey a comic. 'Must have fallen out of your pocket. Tiffany found it in the Spanglemobile –'

'T-Tiffany?!'

'– and brought it to the pizza bar. Whizzeroonie of her, I thought. Told me she made you a Spangle Special à la Bailey. Sounds whizzeroonie too. Now – you going to get undressed or what? The Skipper's already in bed.'

Tiffany certainly didn't waste much time! thought Bailey, stripping to his boxers and getting into bed. Trust me to lose my comic.

'You're frowning again, kiddo,' said Monty, tucking Bailey into bed. 'Hey, I know something that'll cheer you up. Fresh from the restaurant!' He took an apple pie, wrapped in a serviette, from his pocket. 'If you eat something sweet before you go to sleep, you'll have sweet dreams.'

Bailey bit into the pie's crust. Warm, sweet apple trickled down his chin.

'Careful there, kiddo,' warned Monty, walking towards the door. 'The Skipper'll go whacko if you get the sheets dirty. Goodnight, kiddo.' He turned the light off and left.

Now I've got something else to worry about! thought Bailey, munching in the moonlight. Tiffany Spangle!

But negative! I won't worry about anything.

I'll just think about Scribbleboy instead.

The fan club meets tomorrow!

And I will join!

Tomorrow!

TUESDAY

— 9 —

'There it is, Skipper,' announced Bailey.

'Affirmative, Trooper Two.'

'Doesn't look too b-bad, eh, Skipper?'

'Negative, Trooper Two.'

'You want me to hold your hand, Skipper?'

'Affirmative, Trooper Two.'

The Unemployment Office was a large, square, practically windowless building made of – you guessed it! – concrete. Where some of the concrete had fallen away, it had been replaced by corrugated iron, and both the concrete and the corrugated iron were covered with – I bet you're ahead of me on this one – birds' mess, weeds and graffiti. Most of the graffiti read, 'GISS A JOB!'

'R-ready, Skipper?' asked Bailey, stepping forward.

'Ahhh ... now then!' gasped the Skipper, pulling Bailey back. 'Give me an inspection first, Trooper Two. Is my monocle sparkling?'

'Af-affirmative.'

'Feather in my hat fluffy?'

'Affirmative.'

'Moustache not limp and drooping?'

'Negative, Skipper. You're the p-perfect officer and gentleman.'

'An officer and a gentleman!' gasped the Skipper. 'That's all one can hope for in the present circumstances, I suppose. Now – let battle commence!'

They entered the building.

There were hundreds of people milling around.

People reading leaflets, people queuing, people leaning against walls waiting for other people, mothers with crying babies, small children yelling for drinks or crisps, old people with tears in their eyes, people sitting on the floor, and all of them were yelling, cursing, pushing, shoving, smoking, coughing.

And then –

Laughter!

Some people had noticed the Skipper.

'You going to a fancy-dress party or what?' jeered one.

The Skipper clutched Bailey's hand so tight it hurt.

'Don't let them b-bother you, Skipper,' Bailey said, glaring at the people around him.

But the Skipper was trembling all over. 'I don't like this place at all, Trooper Two. It's not shipshape or Bristol fashion in any way! Look! There's a half-eaten sandwich there. Pork luncheon meat if I'm not mistaken – Ah! My monocle!'

The Skipper's monocle had fallen to the ground.

'Where is it?' cried the Skipper, getting to his knees.

CRUNCH!

Someone trod on it!

'Disaster!' The Skipper stared at the crushed glass on the floor.

'G-get up!' Bailey helped the Skipper to his feet. 'Relax!'

'How can I relax, Trooper Two? We're in enemy territory here!'

Someone sneezed near by.

'Germ warfare!' cried the Skipper. 'Have you got your gas-mask, Trooper Two?'

'It's n-not gas, Skip –'

'We've walked into a terrible trap. Yellow alert!'

Suddenly the Skipper was backing towards the door, trembling all over and crying at the top of his voice, 'ABANDON SHIP! MAYDAY! ABANDON SHIP! RETREAT! SOS!'

'Skipper! Please!'

'MISSION ABORTED! ORANGE ALERT!'

Someone laughed and blew smoke into the Skipper's face.

'RED ALERT!' shrieked the Skipper. 'RETREAT!' He ran out of the Unemployment Office.

'C-come back, Skipper!' yelled Bailey, rushing after him.

'MAYDAY!' The Skipper was running across the road.

Cars swerved to miss him.

'SKIPPER!'

By the time Bailey had made it to the other side of the road, the Skipper had disappeared amongst the concrete maze of buildings, and all Bailey could hear was his dad's distant voice crying, 'MAYDAY! SOS! ABANDON SHIP! RETREAT! RETREAT! RETREAT! . . .'

'SK-SKIPPER?' called Bailey.

No response.

'SKIPPER!'

Nothing.

Oh, where is he? thought Bailey. I've been looking for him for over an hour now. He couldn't have gone home! He doesn't know the way back.

'SKIPPER!'

Nothing.

If I wander too far I'm not going to find the way back myself. All these concrete buildings look exactly the same to me. And look at that! An abandoned van! The tyres and windows are missing! What a mess –

'Yeeow!' cried a voice.

Bailey looked all around.

He couldn't see anyone.

'Up here, Uniform Kid!'

Bailey looked up and saw –

A boy standing on top of the van. He was wearing baggy jeans (so baggy, in fact, that the waist was almost round his knees, revealing the boxer shorts beneath), black string vest, baseball cap (turned round the wrong way) and dark glasses.

'Got a question for you, Uniform Kid,' said the boy. 'Now school's out for the summer and the sun's rays are a-raying, you should be out a-laughing and a-playing – Yeeow!' He clapped his hands, pleased with his rhyme. 'What I'm trying to say is, you should be clowning, not frowning – Yeeow!' Another clap.

'I'm not f-f –'

'Let me introduce myself, Uniform Kid. I'm the Main

Man. The Top Dog. The Big Cheese. The Numero Uno. In short, Levi Toot's the name and rapping's my game – Yeeow!' Clap! 'I'm a-rootin' and tootin' today.' He spun round on one leg. 'And I'll tell you something else, Uniform Kid. I know just the thing to get rid of that frown of yours.'

'I'm not f-f –'

'Don't deny, Uniform Kid! You're wearing your frown like a king wears a crown – Yeeow!' Clap! 'And only dancing can get rid of it!'

'D-dancing!'

'Yo!'

'But . . . I've n-never danced!'

'Never danced! No wonder you're frowning as deep as where the moles creep – Yeeow!' Clap! 'If you ain't dancing, you're in trouble, cos all your troubles start to double – Yeeow!' Clap! 'HEY! HIP-HOP!' he yelled suddenly, stomping his foot on top of the van. 'WAKE UP, HIP-HOP! WAKE UP!' Stomp! Stomp! 'WE'VE GOT US A FROWNING UNIFORM KID NEEDS A DOSE OF DANCING! I'VE BEEN GIVING HIM THE PREACHING, NOW WE GOTTA DO SOME TEACHING – YEEEEOOW!!!' Clap!

A boy clambered sleepily out of the back of the van.

Like Levi, he was wearing a baseball cap, black string vest, baggy T-shirt and sunglasses. Unlike Levi, he was very, very short.

'This here's my homeboy, Hip-Hop,' Levi said to Bailey. Then looked at the boy. 'Say hello to Uniform Kid, Hip-Hop.'

'Yo!' mumbled Hip-Hop. 'Chuck-a-boom!'

Bailey frowned and looked at Levi. 'What's chuck-a-boom m-mean?'

'That's the way ol' Hip-Hop speaks,' Levi explained. 'You see, Uniform Kid, we're in a rapping group. I'm the lead rapper. And Hip-Hop here – why, he's one of the musical instruments. He makes some of the best drum-machine noises my ears ever heard, and I've heard the best.'

'What's your g-group called?'

'Levi Toot and the Homeboys. Ain't that a wicked name?'

'I take it w-wicked means good!' said Bailey.

'Wicked means bad.'

'So b-bad means good?'

'Bad means radical.'

'So r-radical means good?'

'Course it does, Uniform Kid! Where you been living?' He looked at Hip-Hop. 'Now, Hip-Hop, my homeboy, you heard what I said, Uniform Kid can't dance, so he's half dead – Yeeow!' Clap!

'Yo! Chuck-a-boom!'

'That's right, Hip-Hop.'

Bailey looked amazed. 'You understand w-what he says!'

'Sure do, Uniform Kid.'

'But . . . how?'

'Takes years of practice, Uniform Kid! Every little inflection of every "chuck" and "a" and "boom" carries meaning. Some people tell me it's like Japanese! But I don't know Japanese from the itching of fleas – Yeeow!' Clap! 'Now, enough of this rapping! It's dancing time!

Hip-Hop, show Uniform Kid how to spin on his back!'

And suddenly Hip-Hop was wide awake and on the floor. Laying on his back. Legs curled up. And . . .

Spinning!

I'm getting dizzy just looking at him, thought Bailey.

'Yeeow!' cried Levi, laughing with joy. 'Watch him go! Yo! Do it, Hip-Hop, my homeboy! Do it!' Then he looked at Bailey. 'You try, Uniform Kid.'

'I can't!' Bailey exclaimed. 'I mean, I'd love to learn how to sp-spin on my back. Really I w-would. But not n-now. I'm looking for the Skipper.'

'The Kipper?'

'*Skipper!* He's r-run away! I've got to find him!'

'Say no more, Uniform Kid. Your Kipper wearing a hat with a feather in?'

'Affirm – I mean, yes!'

'Then your searching is a-over, Uniform Kid. I can see almost the whole neighbourhood from up here, and your Kipper –'

'*Skipper!*'

'– is over there!' Levi pointed. 'In the old garage. Yo! Is that a hamster under his nose?'

'Neg – I mean, no. It's a m-moustache.'

'Most radical moustache I ever seen, Uniform Kid. But, if that's your Kipper, you best get to him quick. Looks like he's mighty upset. Dancing lessons can resume another time, when you ain't distracted and are totally mine – Yeeow!' Clap!

The garage was a ruin. The petrol pumps were buckled and rusty, what was left of the main building was covered in – what else? – birds' mess, weeds and – need I say? – graffiti, and the carwash was nothing more than a rotting iron cage, like the gigantic ribs of some long-dead animal.

The Skipper was sitting in the middle of the carwash, staring straight ahead, his mouth open, trembling.

Shell-shock! thought Bailey. It happens when things get too much for the Skipper. Been happening at least three or four times a week lately.

He rushed up and embraced him. 'You're safe now, Skipper!' And then Bailey saw it!

Or, to be precise, *felt* it!

Behind him!

Like a prowling thing waiting to pounce!

Slowly, he turned –

A Scribble!

On an old chocolate-dispensing machine.

It looked so out of place in the decrepit dullness of the garage. Like something from another planet. Or a monolith from Stonehenge. Except that this was –

Emerald green!

Ruby red!

Sapphire blue!

'Where am I, Trooper Two?' asked the Skipper weakly.

Forget about the Scribble! Bailey thought. Time enough for that later.

'Don't worry about an-anything, Skipper. You're s-safe now. In friendly territory. Can you g-get up?'

'Af-affirmative,' the Skipper replied faintly.

Bailey helped the Skipper to his feet.

'Trooper Two . . . I need –' began the Skipper

'I kn-know what you need,' interrupted Bailey. 'A dose of *Top Gun*.'

— 12 —

Now, I don't know if you're aware of this or not, but there is a movie called *Top Gun*. It stars an actor called Tom Cruise and is about fighter pilots. There are lots of explosions, even more naughty words, some soppy kissing and a pop song that plays in the background, whether people are exploding things, saying naughty words or kissing.

Nothing so special in that, I hear you say.

And you'd be right.

Except for one thing . . .

Top Gun is the Skipper's favourite film. And, what's more, it's the only thing that can revive him when he's suffering from shell-shock.

Bailey sat the Skipper in front of the television set and turned it on. 'Nearly there, Skipper,' he said. He put the video of *Top Gun* in the video player. 'H-hang on!' He pressed 'Play'.

The screen sparkled into life.

'*Top Gun*!' cried the Skipper.

Success! thought Bailey. Look at him! It's as if he's in the movie.

'Evasive action! Quick, pilot! That's it.' The Skipper

twisted and turned in the armchair. 'Look out for that cloud! Watch out!'

Bailey glanced at his watch.

5.00!

The Scribbleboy Fan Club meets at 5.30, he thought. Don't want to be late.

'Look out, Trooper Two!' The Skipper grabbed hold of Bailey and held him very tight. 'I've got to make a drastic move to avoid that mountain. Can you see it, Trooper Two?'

'Af-affirmative, Skipper.'

'Here goes!' The Skipper clutched Bailey even tighter. 'Phew! That was close, Trooper Two.'

Bailey tried to struggle free. 'Sk-Skipper!'

'Enemy aircraft!' cried the Skipper, grabbing hold of Bailey tighter than ever. 'Hold on, Trooper Two!'

'But I've got to p-pop out, Skipper.'

'Pop out!' cried the Skipper, his eyes glued to the screen. 'How can you? We're in a plane.'

Bailey thought quickly.

'I'm wearing a parachute, Skipper!'

'And what do you want to parachute out for?'

'To . . . do some more r-reconnaissance.'

'Ah! Good idea, Trooper Two! But don't forget, if you get captured by the enemy, don't tell them a thing.'

'Af-affirmative, Skipper.' He went to get up, but the Skipper still held him. 'You'll have to eject me, Skipper.'

'Oh . . . of course, Trooper Two. I'll give you a countdown. Ready?'

'Af-affirmative, Skipper.'

'Three! Two! One! . . . EJECT!!!'

— 13 —

I should be nearly there by now! thought Bailey, studying the directions in the letter. I've walked to the back of my flats and turned left, and now I'm walking down the Big Road – What's that? Oh, a video store. Must be where Monty rented *Top Gun*. It's called Emporium Video. I like all the little fancy lights round the window . . . And look! Over there! Pizza Most Yum-Yum, where Monty works. Hope he doesn't see me. Keep walking, keep walking . . . Wait! What's that?

A large building, completely surrounded by a fence of corrugated iron, was to Bailey's right. On the corrugated iron was a bright red 'S' and then an arrow pointing.

'S' for Scribbleboy, thought Bailey. This must be it!

His heart was beating very fast.

A few steps further on was another arrow.

Then another . . .

Another . . .

Then, suddenly, they stopped.

Where do I go now? I'm surely not expected to climb over the fence – Wait! What's this?

Where the arrows ended, the corrugated iron had come loose.

It opened as easily as a door.

Bailey went inside.

Now he could see the building clearly and – yes! – it did look a little like a cinema.

On top of the building was a green dome. The walls – a mixture of brick and concrete – were mostly cracked, and covered, of course, in graffiti. There were broken neon lights and boarded-up FIRE EXITS and stone steps leading up to the main doors. The name of the cinema was written in unlit neon across the entrance: THE PAVILION. There were hundreds of tattered film posters still stuck to the walls and, on top of these posters, the red arrows started once again.

They pointed to the main entrance.

Bailey walked up the stone steps.

His heart was beating faster and faster.

On one of the doors was written 'S'!

Here goes! thought Bailey, pushing the door open and stepping inside.

Mega-spooky! he thought. That's where they once sold tickets! And there, the kiosk where they sold fizzy drinks and popcorn! And there, some more film posters! Probably the last films the cinema ever showed. Let's have a look . . . *Doctor Jekyll and Mr Hyde*. I think I've seen that on TV. It's about a doctor who drinks a magic potion and changes into a very nasty piece of work. What's this? *Superman*. Oh, I've read about him in my comics. And what's this one? *Pinocchio*. I've seen that one on video. It's for small kids really. Not enough explosions for my liking.

This place must have looked mega-posh once. Now everything's ruined. Broken glass everywhere too. Better be careful where I walk . . .

What's that? An 'S'! On the doors leading into the auditorium! This is it!

Bailey went inside.

Ultra-mega-spooky! he thought.

There were a few holes in the ceiling, letting in shafts of sunlight.

And, in this light, Bailey could see –

Rows of seats! All covered in dust. And there, the screen the films were projected on! And the curtain! Moth-eaten and mouldy. What a totally unshipshape and unBristol fashion place. And where are all the Scribbleboy fans? The letter said there were hundreds. Probably thousands.

He looked at his watch!

5.40. They should be here by now!

'H-hello?' he called.

No response.

'Hello?'

Still nothing.

It's a trick! he thought. There is no Scribbleboy Fan Club!

He kicked one of the seats in anger.

It's not fair to play tricks on people like this! It's just not fair!

Bailey kicked the chair so hard it started to fall apart.

I needed Scribbleboy! he thought, kicking and kicking.

And he was just about to storm out of the place when –

'Scribbletations, New Kid!' said a voice.

— **14** —

A side door leading to the street (marked FIRE EXIT) had opened.

A figure was silhouetted in the doorway.

The sunlight's dazzling my eyes! thought Bailey. Can't see who it is! But it's a boy's voice. And he said 'Scribbletations!' So it must be –

'Knew you'd come, New Kid,' the boy was saying, struggling to shut the door behind him. 'First time I saw you I thought, "There goes a Scribbler if ever I saw one." Takes one to know one as they say. Oh, pesky door!'

Bailey couldn't see exactly what the problem was, but he could hear a lot of clanking and clunking. He took a step forward to help.

'No, no, no, New Kid!' the boy cried. 'I can close a door by myself, thank you very much.' More clanking! 'Oh, by the way, New Kid, a million apologies for being late. Wasn't my fault. Roadworks down by the traffic-lights. Meant I had to make a detour.' The door clanged shut. 'Success!'

Bailey blinked a few times, adjusting his eyes to the semidarkness once more, then saw –

A boy about eleven years old, thin, pale, with large brown eyes. He was wearing a green anorak, a white button-up shirt, open at the collar, corduroy trousers and slippers. His hair was jet-black and very curly.

Bailey's first thought was: he's very short.

His second was: negative, not short. He's sitting down.

The third: why's the chair on wheels?

Then he realized: the boy was in a wheelchair.

'Welcome, welcome, welcome, New Kid!' cried the boy, approaching Bailey. 'This *is* exciting! Ain't you excited? I am!' He flicked hair from his eyes. 'Oh, where to start? Aha! I know! The introductions.' He took a deep breath. 'My name is Ziggy Fuzz and, as the President of the Scribbleboy Fan Club, may I welcome you to . . . well, the fan club.'

A smile was all Bailey could manage at this moment.

'Oh, it's just too totally scribbledacious for words!' bubbled Ziggy. 'The Scribbleboy Fan Club is growing from strength to strength.'

'But w-where is it?' asked Bailey.

'Where's what, New Kid?'

'The f-fan club.'

'Here, of course.'

'But . . . where are all the m-members?'

'You're looking at them!'

'W-where?'

'Me and you, New Kid.'

'But . . . your letter said there were h-hundreds.'

'A slight exaggeration, New Kid. When I said hundreds, what I really meant was . . . one.'

'One?'

'Me!'

'Th-that's all?'

'But now there's you, New Kid. Which means the fan club has doubled in size in the last few seconds. Not many fan clubs can say that now, can they?'

'I . . . suppose n-not.'

'Oh, New Kid, I just knew there must be someone out there like me. Somebody who'd feel like I do when they looked at the Scribbles. I knew I couldn't be alone! I just knew it! Wheeeee!' He spun round and round in the wheelchair.

Bailey started to back away, towards the exit.

'What's wrong, New Kid?' Ziggy had stopped spinning, sensing Bailey's movement.

'Well . . .'

'You're disappointed?'

'It's n-not that.'

'What then?'

'I just imagined it all to be . . . d-different.'

'So you *are* disappointed. I knew it! You shouldn't lie to me. Oh . . . *please* don't go!'

'I'm not.'

'Lying again!'

'Well, you're a fine one to t-talk!' Bailey snapped

angrily. 'Who was it that t-told me there were hundreds of members in the fan club? If not thousands! Who was it that b-built my hopes up? Now I'm here and . . . there's nothing. Just a filthy wreck of a b-building and . . . and . . .'

'Me,' said Ziggy softly. 'What a disappointment, eh?'

'I d-didn't mean it like that.' Bailey stopped backing away. 'There's nothing wr-wrong with you.'

'Lying again!'

'I'm not,' maintained Bailey, stepping forward.

'Don't worry,' said Ziggy. 'I'm used to it. Who am I? Nothing. I can't dance and rap like all the others kids around here. After all, I'm just an anorak in a wheelchair –'

'Don't say that –'

'But let me tell you this, New Kid! It was *me*! *Me*! Ziggy Fuzz, who first discovered the Scribbles. It was *me* who gradually pieced together the Legend of Scribbleboy. It was *me* who started the Scribbleboy Fan Club. And it's been *me* – *me alone!* – who kept the name of Scribbleboy alive!' He wheeled closer, his brown eyes glinting like sunlight through bottled Coke. 'But now there's *you*, New Kid. *You're* a Scribbler through and through. And this fan club might not be all you want it to be. And I might not be your idea of a perfect President. But I am still the only fellow Scribbler you've got in the whole neighbourhood. So . . . let me tell you the Legend of Scribbleboy.' He took a deep breath. 'What I'm trying to say is – stay, New Kid! Please! Stay!'

Bailey stared at Ziggy.

Ziggy stared at Bailey.

Then . . .

'Tell me, President,' said Bailey, sitting on one of the old cinema seats. 'Tell me the Legend of Scribbleboy.'

— 15 —

'Once,' began Ziggy, smiling, 'the neighbourhood was nothing but grey. Grey buildings, grey roads, grey playgrounds and grey schools. And this grey was –'

'Concrete!' interrupted Bailey.

'Concrete, New Kid! Exactly! And everyone in the neighbourhood lived in this concrete greyness, because they had no choice. Oh – I know what you're thinking, New Kid. Didn't they complain? And the answer is – at first, yes! But then, gradually, they got used to concrete. They forgot there was anything else. In the end, they believed the only colour the neighbourhood could ever be was grey.'

'But it's n-not!'

'You're right, New Kid. But do you know why you know that?'

'Wh-why?'

'Because you're a kid! You see, New Kid, it's the *grown-ups* who get used to the grey. It's the grown-ups who believe grey is the only colour.'

'But the kids d-didn't.'

'No way! The kids knew there must be something else. And the kids would wish every chance they got. They'd wish for something or someone to put an end to the grey.'

'Scribbleboy!' interrupted Bailey eagerly.

'Oh, please don't rush ahead!' sighed Ziggy. 'Let me tell the legend in my own way!'

'S-Sorry,' said Bailey. 'So ... what happened next?'

Ziggy took a deep breath. 'Well, one day, on a concrete wall, the kids saw –'

BEEP! BEEP!

'Oh, pesky-pesky!' muttered Ziggy irritably. He took a mobile phone from his pocket. 'What, Ma?' he said into it. 'I told you not to bother me. Yes, I did see the roadworks. No, they weren't a problem.' He looked at Bailey and rolled his eyes, mouthing, 'Sorry, New Kid.' A moment later he said goodbye and put the phone back in his pocket. 'My ma, New Kid. Always phones at the worst possible time. Now ... where was I?'

'One day on a c-concrete wall –'

'Ah! Yes!' said Ziggy excitedly. 'This is where it gets *really* interesting.' He took another deep breath, then continued, 'One day, on a concrete wall, the kids saw the most amazing colours. Emerald green. Ruby red. Sapphire blue. And the most dazzling shapes –'

'C-comets!'

'Exactly, New Kid.'

'And st-stars!'

'Exactly!'

'Then it was a Scribble!'

'Exactly, New Kid. That's what the kids of the neighbourhood called it! A Scribble! And the mysterious artist who had done it – whoever he was – they named –'

'Scribbleboy!'

'Exactly, New Kid. Word spread like wildfire amongst all the kids. "Scribbleboy is here!" they cried. "He's going to take away the grey! He's going to make the concrete beautiful! Scribbleboy is here! Scribbleboy is here!"'

'Scribbleboy is h-here!' echoed Bailey, breathless with excitement. 'Oh, I know j-just how those kids must have felt, Ziggy. Seeing a Scribble for the first t-time!' He looked Ziggy in the eye. 'You know, Ziggy, I fainted when I saw the one in the playground.'

'Happens to us all at first, New Kid.'

'It d-does?'

'Sure! In the old days, kids who saw the Scribbles were fainting all over the place. But they got used to it. And so will you.'

'It's d-difficult to imagine *ever* getting used to it. Tell me, Ziggy, how many Scribbles did Scribbleboy scribble in total?'

'Oh, he must have done hundreds. If not thousands. You see, it was Scribbleboy's mission to cover every square centimetre of concrete with Scribbles. But ... well, I'm afraid to say, most of the Scribbles have been destroyed over the years. Now there's only four left. The one in the playground –'

'And I've seen another! In the g-garage.'

'That's the smallest Scribble, New Kid.'

'Wh-where's the biggest?'

'Here, New Kid!'

'Here?' Bailey's head started pounding. 'But ... where?'

'Through that Fire Exit. It covers most of the back wall of the cinema.'

Bailey jumped to his feet. 'I've got to see it now, Ziggy!' he cried. 'NOW!'

— 16 —

Emerald green!

Ruby red!

Sapphire blue!

Comets.

Stars.

'Scribblewonderful or what, New Kid?'

'My name's Bailey, Ziggy. Please don't call me New Kid any more.'

'Sure, New Kid – I mean, Bailey. By the way, how do you feel? I mean, how's the Scribble affecting you? Feel like fainting?'

'I'm a little light-headed, Ziggy.'

'Breathe deeply.'

Bailey did so, then asked, 'Oh, Ziggy, tell me! Did anyone ever actually s-see Scribbleboy?'

'For a long time, no,' replied Ziggy. 'Nobody knew who Scribbleboy was. Or where he came from. Or where he hid all his paints. Kids told stories of hearing the sound of spray-paint at night. Or of seeing a shadowy figure running into even darker shadows. But Scribbleboy remained a mystery. Like UFOs or the Loch Ness Monster. Grown-ups, of course, didn't believe in him! But the kids did! And then ... there was rumour of a sighting!'

'Where?' panted Bailey. 'When?'

'At night, of course. All the Scribbles were done at night.' Ziggy's eyes filled with wonder. 'Scribbleboy was seen standing on the roof of a block of flats. He was silhouetted against a full moon.'

'W-what did he look like, Ziggy?'

'He was wearing a cap and a jacket. Both covered in Scribbles. And there was a belt with cans of paint hanging from it. And in each hand he held a can. He was spraying them into the air, as if he wanted to paint the heavens themselves.'

Bailey trembled with ecstasy. 'Oh, Ziggy, tell me!' he said. 'What happened to Scribbleboy? Why did he stop scribbling? Why did he desert us and let the concrete win?'

'No one knows, Bailey. Not for sure. One day the Scribbles just stopped. And no one saw Scribbleboy any more.' Ziggy sighed, deep and sad. 'For a while the kids continued to hope. They wished for his return. But their wishes did not come true. And then ... well, the years passed. One by one the kids became grown-ups. They forgot how much the Scribbles had meant to them. Forgot to hope. Forgot Scribbleboy.'

There was a long silence.

'I want him b-back, Ziggy,' sighed Bailey, his voice breaking.

'Oh, don't upset yourself too much, Bailey,' insisted Ziggy, concerned for his new friend. 'It's not the end of the legend yet.'

'It's n-not?'

'Listen! The legend goes that, one day, Scribbleboy will return. He will come back to the kids of the neighbourhood, stand on the roof of the block of flats where he was seen, and cry, "MY NAME IS SCRIBBLEBOY AND I'M BACK TO SCRIBBLE!"'

'I am Scribbleboy and I'm back to scribble!' echoed Bailey, relishing the sound of every word. 'And tell me, Ziggy, do we know where this b-block of flats is?'

'My dear fellow Scribbler,' said Ziggy, grinning wider than ever, 'Scribbleboy was seen on top of the flats where *you* live!'

— 17 —

'Oh, Ziggy!' cried Bailey, pacing round and round with excitement. 'This feeling is t-too good. I haven't felt this happy in . . . well, not ever! How many other kids have you told, Ziggy?'

'Well . . . to be honest – just one.'

'One!' gasped Bailey. 'Who?'

'A boy called Levi Toot!'

'Levi Toot?' gasped Bailey. 'I've met him. What did he d-do?'

'He laughed at me. So I never tried again.'

'But we've *got* to try again, Ziggy! We c-can't keep Scribbleboy to ourselves! All the kids of the neighbourhood have a right to know. Perhaps . . . perhaps we've got to find ways of making the fan club more . . . well, more interesting.'

'How do you mean, Bailey?'

'Let's see . . . ' Thinking and pacing. 'Well, like the th-thing that you've already invented. Calling ourselves Scribblers. Saying "Scribbletations!" But it . . . it can be s-so much *more*, Ziggy.'

'How, Bailey?'

'Well . . . when one Scribbler meets another they should salute as well.'

'A salute!' cried Ziggy, getting caught up in Bailey's excitement now. 'A Scribblefabulous idea! But what kind of salute?'

Bailey continued thinking and pacing.

Ziggy started thinking and wheeling.

Then . . .

'Got it!' cried Bailey. 'It has to do with the letter "S". "S" for Scribbleboy, obviously. Like the "S"s you p-painted all round the c-corrugated iron to direct people into this b-building. Look, Ziggy! If you curve the thumb and f-forefinger of one hand so it makes a letter "C" – like this . . . '

'Got it,' said Ziggy, carefully copying Bailey.

'Now, if you do the same with the other hand: thumb and forefinger into the letter "C" . . . '

'Got it! Got it!'

'Now look! Put the thumb of one hand touching the forefinger of the other – like this! And what do you see?'

'The letter "S"!'

'The Scribbleboy salute!'

'Scribbletations, Scribbler!' said Ziggy, giving the salute.

'Scribbletations, Scribbler!' said Bailey, returning the salute.

The two boys spun round and round in excitement.

'Oh, it's so scribbledacious!' cried Ziggy.

'Scribblefabulous, Ziggy.'

'Scribblewonderful, Bailey.'

'Of course! The words, Ziggy!' Bailey cried. 'We can do m-more with the words! Listen to this ... *un*scribbledacious!'

'For something that's not scribbledacious!'

'Affirmative, Ziggy! And ... *un*scribblefabulous!'

'For something that's not scribblefabulous!'

'*Un*scribblewonderful, Ziggy!'

'Something that's not scribblewonderful!'

'Affirmative, Ziggy, affirmative! Oh, and there's so m-much else we could do! I just need time to th-think of it. One thing I do know – we've got to clean this p-place!'

'Clean it?'

Bailey nodded. 'It n-needs a bottle of disinfectant. And some f-furniture polish. There's cupboards full of the stuff at home. The Skipper – I mean, my dad – won't m-miss a few. I'll try to get a couple of air f-fresheners as well.'

'I'll bring a broom!'

'And a duster?'

'You got it!'

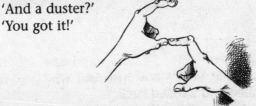

'Tomorrow we'll start making the meeting p-place of Scribbleboy Fan Club totally shipshape and Bristol fashion.'

'But, Bailey – the fan club only meets once a week –'

'Not any longer, Ziggy. From n-now on, it meets every day.'

'Every day?'

'All day!'

'All day? Oh yes, yes! And at what time?'

'Let's see. After breakfast. How about ten o'clock?'

'Yes! Yes! Every day at ten o'clock –'

BEEP! BEEP!

'Pesky-pesky ... ' Ziggy answered the phone. 'What now, Ma? Yes ... all right, all right ... I'll be right there ...' He put the phone back in his pocket. 'I've got to go, fellow Scribbler. Ma says dinner's ready.'

'Dinner!' cried Bailey, suddenly looking at his watch. 'I best be g-going myself, otherwise I'll be late! Can you get h-home all right, Zig?'

'Yes, yes, yes, Bay. Don't worry about me.' And then he gave the salute. 'Scribbletations, Scribbler!'

'Scribbletations, Scribbler!'

— 18 —

'You're late, Trooper Two.'

'Sorry, Sk-Skipper.'

Bailey glanced at Monty and winked.

Monty smiled and winked back.

'Don't think I didn't notice,' the Skipper continued. 'A good commanding officer – like myself – notices everything. Look at you, Trooper Two. Panting like a hippopot –'

'Give it a rest, Skip,' sighed Monty. 'I think we've all got the point.'

'Oh ... er, affirmative, Trooper One.'

'Besides,' continued Monty, 'we've got more

important things to talk about, Skip. Like you not signing on. What happened, exactly?'

'I told you, Trooper One,' mumbled the Skipper, looking timidly at his fishfingers and twiddling his moustache. 'Germ warfare. We were lucky to get out with our lives.'

'Germ warfare? Oh, Skip, listen to me, this is really unwhizzeroonie . . .'

Bailey's mind drifted off, back to the old cinema, to Ziggy, and the Legend of Scribbleboy. Usually, he listened intently to everything the Skipper and Monty said. But tonight was different. Tonight he was thinking –

A newsletter! That's what we've got to start! A newsletter to let all the other kids know about Scribbleboy. The newsletter will tell the legend. And list all the remaining Scribbles –

'Hear that, kiddo?'

'Oh, what, Mont? I was miles away.'

'I'm going to take the Skipper to the Unemployment Office tomorrow! He's got to sign on somehow. By the way, why are you still sitting at the table?'

It was only then Bailey realized that, not only was dinner over, but the washing-up had been done, and the Skipper was sitting out in the hall, watching the phone.

Time flies when I'm thinking about Scribbleboy! thought Bailey.

'I'll bring you back an apple pie and a slice of pizza later,' whispered Monty. 'You hardly ate any dinner.' He peered closer. 'You know something? Tiffany's right.' He rubbed his thumb between Bailey's eyebrows. 'Your frown doesn't look so deep – oh, I nearly forgot, she made me one of her specials today!' He walked out into the hall.

'She ... *what*?!' Bailey chased after him. 'Tiffany m-m-made you a Special?'

'Affirmative, kiddo.'

'But that means she t-touched your tongue!'

'Affirmative, kiddo.'

'But how c-could you let her?'

'Why not? She touched yours.'

'That's different!'

'Why?'

'Just is!'

Monty opened the front door. 'Stop brooding, kiddo,' he said, then winked and left.

'Ring!' murmured the Skipper, staring at the phone. 'Oh, ring, ring, ring!'

Bailey went to his room and flopped down on the bed.

I'm not going to think about any of them! he thought. Not Skipper! Not Tiffany! Not Mum! All I want to think about is ... Scribbleboy.

WEDNESDAY

— 19 —

'A . . . news *what?*' asked Ziggy

'News*letter*,' explained Bailey. 'Most fan clubs have them. Open the bag wider, Zig!'

They'd met at 10.00, as arranged, and had started cleaning the auditorium of the cinema. Ziggy had brought a broom, duster and bin-bags; Bailey had disinfectant, furniture polish and air-fresheners.

They'd cleaned most of the seats, and now Bailey was sweeping each aisle in turn.

Ziggy waited at the end of the aisle, bin-bag at the ready.

'And what do we put in this newsletter, Bay?'

'We'll tell the other kids the Legend of Scribbleboy, to begin with. And where all the Scribbles can be found. And after that the newsletters will keep them informed of all the Scribble news as it happens.'

'*Scribblenews*!' cried Ziggy. 'That's what we'll call the newsletter, Bay! *Scribblenews*!'

'Scribbledacious, Zig!'

'Mega-scribbledacious, Bay!'

'Ultra-mega-scribbledacious, Zig!'

'Totally-ultra-mega-scribbledacious, Bay!'

BEEP! BEEP!

'Oh, pesky-pesky!' Ziggy took the mobile phone from his pocket. 'What now, Ma?'

Bailey took the bin-bag from Ziggy, popped in some more tin cans and chocolate wrappers, then took it outside.

This is the eleventh bag! he thought, throwing it on a pile. And it's still far from shipshape and Bristol fashion inside.

Ting-a-ling-a-ting-a-ting.

That sounds like an ice-cream van!

He peered through a gap in the fence.

Tiffany's Spanglemobile was driving slowly down the street.

It stopped outside –

Pizza Most Yum-Yum! Where Monty works! thought Bailey. He must be able to hear her bells! I was right! There he is! Rushing out on to the street. Tiffany's standing at the serving hatch. Monty's rushing up to the van. Tiffany's leaning forward. They're getting close. Closer. And ...

They're kissing!

Bailey blinked in disbelief.

A few kids were standing by the van, waiting to be served.

But they didn't get served. Because –

They're still kissing! thought Bailey. Look at them! They'll suffocate if they don't come up for air soon. Those poor kids'll never get their ice-cream at this rate.

Wait a minute! Is that –? No! It can't be!

He rushed to a large crack to get a better look.

Tiffany's hair is spinning! While she's kissing Monty! How can she manage that? Even the kids are gawping in disbelief! But Tiffany said her hair only spun when she got excited! Oh, I don't like this at all! Where will it end? Monty might leave home to live with Tiffany. I'll be alone with the Skipper. That'll never do –

'Bay!' Ziggy called from inside. 'Where are you?'

For a moment Bailey didn't want to stop watching Monty and Tiffany.

But then –

Forget about them! he thought. I don't care what happens . . . not outside! I'm *inside* now! *Inside* the world of Scribbleboy! I'm a Scribbler!

Bailey rushed back into the auditorium.

'Oh, Zig! Zig!' he cried. 'I've still got one Scribble left to see. I've seen the one in the playground. And the one on the dispenser machine. And the one here. Now I've got to see the fourth one!'

'What . . . right *now*?'

'This in-instant, Zig!'

'But what about the cleaning?'

'I can't w-wait, Zig!'

'But –'

'NOW, ZIG! NOOOWWW!!!'

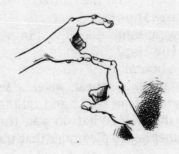

— 51 —

'Scribbledacious, Zig!'

'Mega-scribbledacious, Bay!'

'Ultra-mega-scribbledacious, Zig!'

'Totally-ultra-mega-scribbledacious, Bay!'

The Scribble covered the length of a low concrete wall.

'This wall went round a h-house once,' said Bailey, studying the site as if it were the remains of a long-lost civilization. 'That's w-what that pile of bricks used to be.' He started walking over the debris of the house. 'W-we used to live in a h-house made of bricks,' he said softly. 'Our k-kitchen was about here! Fridge – here! Microwave – here! And there was a w-window – about here!' He touched the space in front of him. 'And when I looked out I could see a g-garden . . .'

Ziggy wheeled closer and lent his elbows on the concrete wall. 'What else, Bay?'

'I c-can smell something!' Bailey gasped. 'Shepherd's pie! Mum's cooking shepherd's pie! That's my f-favourite dish in the whole world! Mum! How long to dinner –?'

'Yo! Uniform Kid!'

Levi Toot strode round the corner.

Beside him was Hip-Hop.

'Now I've seen some doolally things in my time. Ain't that so, Hip-Hop?'

'Yo! Chuck-a-boom!'

'But I ain't never – repeat: *never* – seen someone scarpering over a pile of bricks and calling out, "Mum! How long to dinner?" What do you think, Uniform Kid? You got shepherd's pie under that trash, steaming minced beef and buttery mash – Yeeow!' He slapped hands with Hip-Hop. Then suddenly looked all round. 'Hey, Hip-Hop! We've gone and lost Be-Bop again.'

'Yo! Chuck-a-boom!'

'Every time that homeboy dances he goes backwards.' Then he called, 'BE-BOP! IT'S THE MAIN MAN CALLING YOU! THE TOP DOG! THE BIG CHEESE! THE NUMERO UNO! COME AND JOIN US, QUICK! HIP-HOP AND ME ARE SEEING SOME DOOLALLY THING WITH THE UNIFORM KID AND THE ANORAK KID!'

Bailey looked at Ziggy. 'Anorak Kid?'

'What he calls me,' sighed Ziggy. 'Pathetic, if you ask me. Perhaps we should call him Baggy-Jeans-and-Pants-Showing Kid.'

'These are not *pants*!' declared Levi, glaring at Ziggy. 'They're *boxers*! And showing off a little boxer is wicked.'

'Only if wicked means "totally moronic",' commented Ziggy.

'You've got no style, Anorak Kid.'

'And you've got no belt to hold your jeans up.'

The argument would have continued were it not for a boy rushing up –

'Yo! Skoom-sha-skoom!'

'There you are, Be-Bop!' said Levi to the boy. 'And I've warned you before: you've got to go *forwards* sometimes when you're jiving, otherwise you ain't never going to be arriving – Yeeow!' Clap! Levi looked at Bailey. 'This here's Be-Bop, Uniform Kid. He's part of my group too. Another one of my most wicked backing singers. He's Hip-Hop's brother.'

'They're *so* a-alike,' said Bailey, 'I can't tell them apart.'

'But they're totally different, Uniform Kid!' exclaimed Levi. 'Look! Hip-Hop has longer eyelashes! And Be-Bop has longer fingernails. Also Hip-Hop only raps –'

'Yo! Chuck-a-boom!'

'And Be-Bop only raps –'

'Yo! Skoom-sha-skoom!'

'And, what's more, Be-Bop here does the baddest moon-dancing on the planet! Show the Uniform Kid, Be-Bop!'

'Yo! Skoom-sha-skoom!'

And Be-Bop started to give the impression of walking forwards while, in effect, moving backwards.

'Am-amazing!' gasped Bailey. 'Don't you think so, Zig?'

'Only if "amazing" means "what's the point?"' commented Ziggy.

'Anorak Kid wouldn't know good dancing if it stomped on his head,' said Levi. 'And that reminds me,

Uniform Kid. Your dancing lessons! You ran away yesterday to find your Kipper –'

'Skipper!' corrected Bailey. 'And I've still got m-more important things to think about, Levi.'

'What can be more important than dancing?' gasped Levi.

'This!' declared Bailey, pointing at the wall. 'It's a S-Scribble. Scribbled by Scribbleboy –'

— 54 —

And, suddenly, Levi was laughing.

And Hip-Hop.

And Be-Bop.

'It's t-true!' exclaimed Bailey.

'Don't tell me you've fallen for all the Anorak Kid's stuff, Uniform Kid?' said Levi through his laughter. 'Anorak Kid tried to persuade me once. I laughed then – Ha! And I'm laughing now – Ha! Ha! Come on, homeboys, let's get going! This madness might be ... *contagious*! Ha! Ha! Ha!'

'Ha! Chuck-a-boom! Ha!'

'Ha! Skoom-sha-skoom! Ha!'

And they walked away, their laughter echoing after them.

'I'm s-sorry, Zig,' sighed Bailey. 'I thought if we could get Levi to believe in Scribbleboy then all the kids in the neighbourhood would follow.'

'We don't need them, Bay! All we need is you and me –'

BEEP! BEEP!

'Oh, pesky-pesky!' Ziggy snatched the mobile phone from his pocket. 'What is it, Ma? No, this is not a good time to call. Yes, I *am* busy! I'm showing Bailey the Scribble –'

Bailey shot Ziggy a look.

Ziggy looked awkward.

He's talking to his mum about the Scribble! thought Bailey. I thought no grown-up was supposed to know!

'Got to go, Ma!' Ziggy put the phone back in his pocket.

'You *lied* to m-me!' said Bailey, stamping his foot.

'I didn't –'

'You did! Don't t-tell grown-ups, you said! And I t-take it your ma *is* a grown-up?'

'Yes, but –'

'I don't like b-being lied to! It's over, Zig! You hear me? Over! W-we're not f-friends any more!'

And with that, Bailey stormed off.

— 21 —

'Come back, Bay!'

'No!'

'I can't keep up with you!'

'Don't t-try!'

'But I want to explain!'

'I don't w-want you to!'

'Oh, slow down, Bay! Please! My wheelchair's too slow.'

'Not my p-problem!'

'But I'm your fellow Scribbler.'

'You're not my f-fellow anything.'

'Don't cross the road!'

'I can c-cross the road if I like.'

'But I can't get down the kerb, Bay.'

'S-so?'

'But, Bay! Please! – Ahhhhh!'

'Oh, d-do shut up!'

'Help, Bay! Help!'

'You can't t-trick me into –'

'I'm not, Bay! Help! I've fallen over!'

'W-what? Zig! You're lying in the g-gutter!'

'Help!'

'I'll be r-right there!'

'Quick! There's a lorry coming!'

'I'm here, Zig! Here! Y-you OK?'

'Just a little dusty.'

'N-nothing broken?'

'No, Bay. But where's my mobile phone? Bay! Look! It's there in the road!'

'I'll g-get it, Zig.'

'No! Don't. There's a lorry coming!'

'But there's t-time, Zig.'

'Leave it! Too risky –'

CRUNCH!

'Oh . . . Zig! The lorry's sq-squashed your phone!'

'I can see that, Bay.'

'I'm s-sorry, Zig.'

'Don't blame yourself, Bay. It was an accident.'

'It *wasn't* an accident! It was m-my fault! Me and my

temper – oh, I don't know what gets into me sometimes. It's just th-that – well, when I heard you telling your ma –'

'Bay, *please* let me explain –'

'You don't h-have to –'

'I *do*! You see, I *have* to tell my ma! I've got no choice. Who do you think put my letter through your letterbox?'

'You m-mean –?'

'Of course, Bay. The lift in your flats never works. And I could never get my wheelchair up those stairs. That's why I tell Ma about Scribbleboy. I need her help in lots of ways most kids can't even imagine. But she understands, Bay. Honestly. I've sworn her to secrecy. She'll never say a word to anyone. I know I should have told you, Bay. And I know it's annoying when the phone rings all the time –'

'It's n-not annoying, Zig. I'd love it if my mum r-rang all the time. In fact, I'd love it if m-my mum rang just once.'

'Why . . . why don't you tell me about it, Bay?'

'What?'

'Your mum! Everything. Like on those chat shows.'

'What . . . like Oprah Winfrey?'

'Exactly! Ma watches them all the time. All those people telling their problems to an audience. Well, I know we haven't got an audience . . . but I can *still* interview you.'

'Oh, I don't know, Zig –'

'It'll be good for you, Bay! Get it off your chest! Let's go to the playground! It'll be nice and quiet there.'

'I'm still n-not sure –'

'Do it as a favour to me, Bay! After all, you were responsible for my phone getting broken!'

'Oh . . . all right, Zig! Anything for a fellow Scribbler!'

'Welcome, ladies and gentleman,' said Ziggy in his best chat-show-host voice, 'to the first edition of *The Ziggy Fuzz Show.*'

They were in the playground now: Bailey sitting on the swing, Ziggy beside him in the wheelchair. The Scribble was like a huge backdrop.

Ziggy grabbed an old tin can and held it like a microphone. 'Today, ladies and gentlemen, we're going to discuss parents. Parents are very strange people, I'm sure you'll agree. They wear embarrassing clothes. Dance like idiots. Cry at soppy films. Rave about popstars you've never heard of. And – strangest of all for us kids to understand – sometimes they leave home. And that is the subject of today's programme. Sometimes, when a parent leaves, us kids don't know the reason. And that gives us a lot to think about. My guest today is someone who had a parent walk out on him. The parent in question was his mum. Ladies and gentlemen, will you please put your hands together for Mr Bailey Silk!'

Both Ziggy and Bailey clapped.

'Mr Silk,' Ziggy went on in his most serious voice, 'let's begin at the beginning, if we may.'

'Af-Affirmative, Mr Fuzz,' said Bailey just as seriously.

'Now, you lived in a house, I believe. Tell me, was it far from here?' He thrust the tin can under Bailey's nose.

'Er . . . negative, Mr Fuzz. I could run there in about f-fifteen minutes if I wanted to.'

'Was it a nice house, Mr Silk?'

'Very nice, Mr Fuzz. I t-told you, it was like the one we saw –'

'But our viewers haven't seen that, have they, Mr Silk? And you lived there with your mum and dad. And your brother, I believe?'

'Affirmative, Mr Fuzz. His n-name is Monty.'

'Were you happy?'

'V-very happy. Mum was manager of a t-television rental shop. Dad ran his own c-cleaning firm. And Monty was going to c-college. He wanted to be a chef. Some nights he would c-cook dinner. The strangest things. Once he cooked . . . oh, I can't say it, Zig. It's too disgusting.'

'What?'

'You'll feel sick, Zig.'

'Tell me! Tell me!'

'Ostrich!'

'Ostrich?! You're joking, Bay.'

'Negative. He cooked ostrich steak with roast p-potatoes, peas and Yorkshire pudding.'

'What did that taste like, Bay?'

'I don't know. I only ate the vegetables. But . . . Mum, *she* ate the ostrich though.'

'She did?' gasped Ziggy. Then, suddenly remembering what they were supposed to be doing, clutched the tin can tighter and returned to his chat-show-host voice. 'So tell me about your mum, Mr Silk. What was she like?'

'Oh . . . she was scribbledacious – oh, can I say scribbledacious, Mr Fuzz?'

'I'm sure everyone in the world knows what scribbledacious means, Mr Silk.'

'Well, that's w-what she was. Totally-ultra-mega-scribbledacious. She was always very smart.'

'So now, Mr Silk, tell us ... what happened? You're happy in your home with your cleaning-firm dad, your crazy-cook brother and your ostrich-eating mother. What went wrong?'

'It s-started about a year ago, I guess,' said Bailey. 'First, Dad lost his j-job.'

'Aha!' Ziggy looked round at the imaginary audience for a response.

'Then Mum lost her j-job.'

'Aha!' More looks.

'There was l-less and less money. Dad had to s-sell the car. Monty had to give up the idea of going to college –'

'No more ostrich.'

'Affirmative. Then we started selling f-furniture. And then ... we had to s-sell the house! And all the time my dad was becoming, well ... he started to act strange.'

'In what way, Mr Silk?'

'Well ... t-talking like he was in the army or navy or airforce. Calling me Trooper Two and Monty Trooper One. Wanting me and Monty to call him Skipper. Saying "Negative" and "Affirmative" instead of "No" and "Yes". And buying f-funny clothes from army-surplus and f-fancy-dress stores. Wanting me to wear my sch-school uniform all the time. And growing a huge moustache. Calling home "HQ". Cooking thick, l-lumpy porridge for breakfast. And watching his f-favourite film, *Top Gun*, over and over again.'

'His favourite film's *Top Gun*?'

'Affirmative.'

'He's crazier than I thought!'

'He's not crazy, Zig!' snapped Bailey angrily. Then,

realizing Ziggy was only joking, he calmed down and continued, 'And then, well ... just over t-two months ago ... ' His voice trailed away.

Ziggy nearly shoved the can up Bailey's nose. 'What happened, Mr Silk?'

'Mum left us! She didn't tell anyone about it. No warning. Nothing. She left a note on my pillow.'

'What did the note say, Mr Silk?'

'That ... she'd ring when she'd sorted herself out. She needed time alone. To think.'

'She needs to be *alone* in order to *think*?'

'That's what the letter said.'

'Parents can be funny things, Mr Silk.'

'Affirmative, Mr Fuzz.'

'And tell me, am I right in assuming this ostrich-eating mum, who needs to be alone just to think, hasn't rung yet?'

'Affirmative, Mr Fuzz.'

Ziggy looked round at the imaginary audience. 'Well, ladies and gentlemen, I'm sure we'd all like to thank Mr Silk for telling us his story. I'm sure we'd all like to say, "Lighten up, Bay!"'

'What?' gasped Bailey, who – to be honest – had expected a more sympathetic response.

'Lighten up! Listen, fellow Scribbler, sometimes parents split up. There's nothing us kids can do about it. So stop moping –'

'I'm not m-moping.'

'You are!'

'Not!'

'Are!'

'Not! Not! Not!'

'Are! Are! Are! And you know how I can tell, Bay? Because that's exactly what I did after *my* pa left *me*!'

Bailey stared at Ziggy. 'Your *dad* left *you*?'

Ziggy nodded. 'And, for a while, I moped and moped. But it didn't last long. Ma cheered me up.'

'But –'

'No "buts", Bay! Come back and see my ma! She'll show you how to cope with things. Come on! Push me, Bay! Push ... MA GLAMROCK, HERE WE COME!'

— 23 —

'Hiya, Ziggy-baby! Where have you been? I've been ringing and ringing! Oh, this must be your new friend! Bailey-baby, is it?'

'Affirmative,' said Bailey.

Ziggy had just pointed at the flat where he lived (a ground-floor concrete cube in a larger concrete cube), when the front door was flung open and out rushed his mother.

Ma Glamrock's hair, which was long and very frizzy, had glitter sprinkled in it, like metallic dandruff. Her eyeshadow was bright blue (and glittery), her lipstick was bright pink (and glittery) and her nail varnish was bright green (and – you guessed it! – glittery). She was wearing tight white hot-pants (with silver stars on), very high platform shoes (which she found difficult to walk in) and the fluffiest angora sweater imaginable (cut in half, to show off her midriff). In fact, she was, without doubt, the fluffiest, frizziest, not to mention glitteriest, person Bailey had ever seen.

'My Ziggy-baby's been telling me all about you, Bailey-baby,' said Ma Glamrock, kissing Bailey on both cheeks. 'Now, Ziggy-baby,' she continued, wagging her finger at her son, 'the phone! I rang! No answer. Why?'

'A . . . lorry ran over it, Ma.'

'A lorry?' Ma Glamrock's eyes went very wide. 'Are you all right? Oh, baby, baby!'

'I'm fine, Ma,' said Ziggy. 'We were just . . . ' He took a deep breath, glanced at Bailey, then lied, 'crossing a road and the phone slipped from my pocket. Before I had a chance to go back for it a lorry came along and – splat!'

'Oooo!' squealed Ma Glamrock. 'My poor baby! I've got goose bumps just thinking about it! Come on, let's get inside! I need a burst of disco to de-goose bump me!'

There was a ramp leading up to the front door for Ziggy's wheelchair.

Bailey pushed him inside and saw –

A mirrorball!

Hanging from the ceiling, sparkling light everywhere.

In fact, everything in the flat seemed to shimmer and shine: the sofa was shiny green plastic, the curtains had rhinestone patterns on them and the wallpaper was covered with silver polka dots. There was also a white portable television, a very fluffy rug, a record player (with records scattered all around) and literally hundreds of lava-lamps.

'Now, what song shall we have?' wondered Ma Glamrock, sorting through her records. 'I've gotta start funking my stuff pretty soon!' She glanced at Bailey. 'Oh, I can tell Bailey-baby don't like disco. Look at that frown!'

'I'm n-not frowning.'

'I can see it from here! That's just the sort of frown Ziggy's pa used to have whenever I strutted my funky stuff.' She shook her head ruefully. 'I like pretty tunes and lovely lyrics, you see. But Pa ... well, Pa couldn't care less about tunes. And as for lyrics – well, he couldn't even write! Where's that letter he wrote? Ah! Here it is! Try not to laugh, Bailey-baby.'

The letter was written with pencil on what looked like old fish-and-chip paper.

DEER MAR GLAMROCK
and ziggy (oF corse)
I stil luv ya boFe.
But I am fedup
wiv livin ere
So I am leavin
Not goin Far thow
Lots a luv
Pa Punkrock

'Pa Punkrock?' gasped Bailey.

'That's the kind of music he likes, Bailey-baby,' explained Ma Glamrock. 'Punk! Ugh! Awful stuff.'

'Where is he n-now?' asked Bailey.

'He's started his own little shop just down the high street,' replied Ma Glamrock. 'Oooo, that reminds me,

Ziggy-baby, you must see Pa Punkrock tomorrow to get another mobile phone.'

'Sure, Ma.'

'And now,' she went on, 'I've got to start disco dancing! Come on, you two. Help me choose a record!'

'Let's get to my room!' Ziggy said, tugging at Bailey's sleeve. 'QUICK!'

— 24 —

The walls in Ziggy's bedroom were covered from top to bottom with photographs of Scribbles.

'There's something I want you to see, Bay.' He took something from a drawer and held it up for Bailey. 'What do you think?'

It was a bright red 'S' on a square of card. The 'S' was decorated with yellow swirls and whirls, a few blue diamonds, a couple of white stars and a green comet.

'What is it, Zig?'

'It's a design for a badge,' replied Ziggy, suddenly very excited. 'The idea came to me last night! I was up most of the night painting! I thought we should make badges for the two of us. To show that we're Scribblers! Scribbledacious idea, eh?'

'Well ...'

'You don't look very excited, Bay.'

'It's not th-that ...'

'Then what?'

'Well ...' said Bailey thoughtfully. 'You haven't used Scribbleboy's favourite shape, have you?'

'And what's his favourite shape?' demanded Ziggy irritably.

'A circle.'

'How do you know?'

'I just do!'

'That's no answer!'

'It is, Zig! Don't get annoyed.'

'I can get annoyed if I want. It's my room! How do you know what Scribbleboy's favourite shape was anyway –?'

'Because I just *do*, Zig. I f-feel it. I'm not trying to c-cause an argument!'

'You are!'

'I'm not!'

'Are!'

'Not!'

'ARE!'

'NOT!'

'Stop this, babies!' Ma Glamrock had rushed into the room. 'Honestly! How can I choose a record with you two bickering away!'

'It's his fault!' accused Ziggy, pointing at Bailey. 'He says my badge is wrong.'

'It *is* wrong!' Bailey stamped his foot.

'Oooo, stop it, please!' cried Ma Glamrock, pressing her hands over her ears. 'You know what's wrong with you two? You take things too seriously. Always frowning and wearing anoraks.'

'I'm n-not wearing an anorak!' Bailey interrupted.

'Not on the outside, Bailey-baby, but inside, believe me, you're anorak through and through. Now, I want you both to come outside with me this instant and have a good old boogie. It's the quickest way to make friends again. Come on!'

'B-boogie?' gasped Bailey. 'But –'

'No buts! If you argue in my house, then you have to do what Ma Glamrock says. And I want to see you strutting your funky stuff immediately. You too, Ziggy-baby!' She went to put on a record.

Bailey stared at Ziggy in disbelief.

And then . . .

BOOM! BOOM!

The record started.

'Eeeeeeooooowwwww!' cried Ma Glamrock, obviously boogieing. Then, 'Come on, you two – it's grooooooveeeee!'

Ziggy said, 'She won't give up till we do.'

BOOM! BOOM!

Sighing resignedly, Ziggy went into the living-room.

Disco dance! thought Bailey with horror. I just can't do it! No way!

'BAILEY-BABY!' cried Ma Glamrock from the other room. 'YOU'VE GOT TO STRUT YOUR STUFF! AND I MEAN NOWWWWW . . . !'

— 25 —

Slowly, Bailey went into the living-room.

Ma Glamrock was spinning round and round, first toppling on her platforms one way, then the other, and with each topple letting out a piercing, 'Oooooooeeeee!'

And Ziggy was –

Dancing! thought Bailey. Wheeling backwards and forwards. Spinning around. Waving his arms in the air. And he's yelling –

'WEEEEE! COME ON, BAY! IT'S FUN ONCE YOU LET YOURSELF GO! OOOOOEEEEE!'

CLUNK!

A lava-lamp fell!

CLUNK!

Another!

'DANCE, BAILEY-BABY!' cried Ma Glamrock, grabbing Bailey's hand and pulling him into the middle of the room. 'COME ON! LET YOURSELF GO! WEEEEE! BOOGIE! OOOOO! SHIMMY, BABY! DISCOOOOO!'

This is horrific! thought Bailey. I can't dance. I don't know how!

BOOM! BOOM!

Bailey's hips started to wiggle.

BOOM! BOOM!

He started to jiggle.

BOOM! BOOM!

He spun around.

BOOM! BOOM!

And then ...

'WEEEEEE!' Bailey cried out.

'THAT'S IT, BAILEY-BABY!'

'THAT'S IT, BAY!'

I'm dancing! thought Bailey. Look at me! I can't help myself. It's like the boom-booming is inside me.

'SCRIBBLEDACIOUS, ZIG!'

'MEGA-SCRIBBLEDACIOUS, BAY!'

'ULTRA-MEGA-SCRIBBLEDACIOUS, ZIG!'

'TOTALLY-ULTRA-MEGA-SCRIBBLEDACIOUS, BAY!'

BOOM! BOOM!

CLUNK!

And suddenly Ma Glamrock flung open the front door.

She rushed outside and danced on the pavement!

'EEEEEOWWWWW!' cried Ziggy, following her.

'EEEEEOWWWWW!' cried Bailey, following Ziggy.

And the three of them danced round and round each other on the pavement.

Neighbours opened windows. Passers-by stopped to gawp. But the dancers didn't care. All they cared about was the –

BOOM! BOOM!

The whole neighbourhood tremored with the disco beat.

Ma Glamrock boogied round Bailey.

Bailey boogied round Ziggy.

Ziggy boogied round both of them.

And they were laughing and squealing when –

'MAYDAY! MAYDAY!'

'SKIPPER!' cried Bailey, suddenly stopping.

'WHAT'S WRONG, BAILEY-BABY?'

'I CAN HEAR THE SKIPPER – PLEASE! TURN THE MUSIC OFF, MA GLAMROCK!'

Ma Glamrock rushed inside the house.

The boom-booming stopped.

'MAYDAY! ABANDON SHIP!' The voice was getting louder and louder. 'SOS! ABANDON MISSION –'

'SKIPPER!' called Bailey. 'WHERE ARE YOU?'

'There!' cried Ziggy, pointing.

Skipper came running round the corner. His face was pale with terror and he was trembling.

Monty was rushing after him.

Bailey dashed to the Skipper, followed by Ziggy and Ma Glamrock.

'It was land-mines, Trooper Two!' cried the Skipper, falling to his knees and grasping at Bailey. 'RED ALERT! RED ALERT!'

'We've got to get him home, kiddo. He's going to be in total shell-shock any second!'

Monty and Bailey helped the Skipper walk along.

'Can I do anything, Bailey-baby?'

'Negative! Thanks for the boogie, Ma Glamrock.'

'Any time, Bailey-baby.'

'I've got to go, Zig.'

'I'll phone you later, Bay.'

'All right, Zig!'

'Don't drag behind, kiddo!'

'Scribblebye, Zig!'

'Scribblebye! A new word!'

'So it is, Zig! Scribblebye, fellow Scribbler.'

'Scribblebye, fellow Scribbler!'

— 26 —

'Got the video, kiddo?'

'Here it is, Mont.'

'Put it in the player then – Don't panic, Skip! Nearly there!'

'*Top Gun*! Mayday! *Top Gun*!'

'So the Skipper didn't sign on again, Mont. Right?'

'Affirmative, kiddo! The Skip goes in and straight away he says, "It's dirty! Not shipshape and Bristol fashion at all –" How's that video coming along, kiddo?'

'Just rewinding, Mont. What about the land-mines he was talking about?'

'A baby had a balloon. And then – BANG! The balloon explodes! "Land-mines," cried the Skip. You can guess the rest – What's wrong, kiddo?'

'The tape's got stuck, Mont!'

'Stuck? It couldn't have!'

'MAYDAY! MAYDAY!'

'Keep calm, Skip. Press "Eject", kiddo.'

'I am, Mont.'

'Press "Play", then!'

'I have! Nothing h-happens!'

'Let's give it a thump! There! Whizzeroonie! The video cassette's coming out!'

'But, Mont – Look! the t-tape's still stuck in the machine!'

'Stuck? Oh no!'

'The tape's unwinding!'

'MAYDAY! MAYDAY!'

'Don't go whacko, Skip! Get it out, kiddo!'

'I can't, Mont.'

'Look, here, give it a tug!'

'Don't, Mont –'

SNAP!

The tape broke!

'MAYDAY!' cried the Skipper, seeing his beloved film ruined.

'Oh, what a mess!' cried Monty. 'We can barely afford to *rent* this tape, let alone pay for a new one!'

Knock! Knock!

Someone at the front door. Who can that be? thought Bailey. We never get visitors.

'I'll get it, Monty. You keep an eye on Skip!'

Bailey went to the front door and opened it.

'Hello, sweetheart,' said Tiffany. 'I've come to see my Monty.'

Tiffany breezed into the living-room. 'Oh, I know what's happened here – another failed attempt to sign on, eh? And a broken *Top Gun*, or do my eyes deceive me?'

Monty's told her everything about us! thought Bailey. How can he? This is . . . *personal* stuff.

'MAYDAY!'

'No, no, no, Skipper, it's not a mayday, because I'm here to help, really I am, sweetheart.' Tiffany grabbed his wrist. 'Let the Doctor of Ice-Cream feel your pulse.'

The Ice-Cream Diagnosis, thought Bailey. She can't do that! The Skipper hates sweet things!

'Mmmm . . . yes, just as I thought . . . chocolate chip . . . now your temperature.' She lay her hand on the Skipper's forehead. 'Mmmm . . . bananas, I think. Sliced bananas with raspberry syrup . . . no! Vanilla! Yes! Now – your tongue, if you please, Skipper.'

The Skipper will *never* let her touch his tongue! thought Bailey.

But, to his surprise, the Skipper – who had calmed down a little since the diagnosis had begun – stuck his tongue out of his own accord.

'Thank you,' said Tiffany, pinching it between her thumb and finger. 'Mmmm . . . yesssss . . . raisins and glacé cherries! Thank you, Skipper. Now, don't go away, anyone. I'll be right back with a Spangle Special à la Skipper!'

And she rushed out of the flat.

Bailey glared at Monty.

'She's only trying to help, kiddo!'

In no time at all, Tiffany had rushed back, holding the largest ice-cream Bailey had ever seen.

'One Spangle Special à la Skipper!' she said, giving it to the Skipper. 'Now lick that, sweetheart, and all your problems will just melt away.'

Slowly, the Skipper licked. A pause.

'Lick again, sweetheart.'

Another lick.

And then . . .

His eyes lit up.

He started to smile.

The ice-cream is working! thought Bailey. Look! He's laughing now. Monty's grabbed Tiffany. Tiffany's hair is spinning and spinning. Everyone's laughing.

Knock! Knock!

I don't believe it! Someone else at the door now!

'I'll g-get it!' growled Bailey.

He went to the front door and –

'Hiya, Bailey-baby, I just had to come,' said Ma Glamrock. 'Your dad needs some disssscooo!'

— 28 —

'D-disco?' gasped Bailey.

Ma Glamrock strode into the flat. 'He'll soon be strutting his funky stuff and all his problems will disappear – Hiya, everyone!' She was in the living-room now. 'I'm Ma Glamrock, the Disco Queen!'

Look at them all! thought Bailey. Chatting away like they've known each other for years and years. What's happening now . . . ? Ma Glamrock waving her disco record in the air . . .

And Tiffany's jumping up and down squealing, 'Disco music is just peachy-dandy!'

Now Ma Glamrock is putting the record on –

BOOM! BOOM! BOOM! BOOM!

'OOOOOEEEEE!' shrieked Ma Glamrock, waving her arms in the air (and, of course, occasionally toppling in her platforms). 'LET'S BOOGIE, SKIPPER-BABY! LIGHTEN UP! SHIMMY AND SHAKE! COME ON! COME ON!'

The Skipper'll never dance! thought Bailey. Eating an ice-cream is one thing. But dancing! Not in a million years!

'BOOGIE, SKIPPER-BABY!'

'BOOGIE, SWEETHEART!'

'BOOGIE, SKIP!'

Look! The Skipper's on his feet! He's swaying from side to side! Don't do it, Skipper! You'll make a fool of yourself!

But it was too late!

The Skipper was dancing.

'THAT'S IT, SKIPPER-BABY!'

'PEACHY-DANDY, SWEETHEART!'

'GOOD ON YOU, SKIP!'

Look at them all! thought Bailey. Laughing and dancing! I don't like this one little bit! All these strangers in my flat! This place is just for me, Monty and Skipper.

RING! RING!

The phone! That'll be Ziggy. Thank Scribbleboy! Someone with sense to talk to.

Bailey picked up the phone. 'Scribbletations!'

'Scribble-what, cherub?' asked his mum.

— 29 —

Where's my voice gone? thought Bailey. I'm opening my mouth, but nothing's coming out! It's me, Mum! Your cherub! Where are you, Mum? When are you coming back?

'Cherub? You there?'

Don't go, Mum! I'm here. It's just that my voice has disappeared.

In the living-room everyone was still dancing and laughing.

'Is that your father I can hear, cherub?' asked his mum.

Mum'll think we're all having a good time, Bailey thought. She'll think we don't need her. Now she'll never come back.

'Sounds like you're having a party, cherub?'

I can feel the prickling in my eyes now. And I don't want to cry. Not in front of Tiffany and Ma Glamrock –

'WHAT'S WRONG, KIDDO?'

Monty's noticed the look on my face. He's coming over.

'Cherub, is that your brother's voice I can hear?'

Bailey thrust the phone at Monty.

Then ran into his room.

He slammed the door so hard he was sure the whole block of flats must have heard it.

'Hello? ... Mum ...?' he heard Monty say. Then louder, 'HEY, YOU LOT, TURN THE MUSIC DOWN IN THERE ... IT'S MUM, SKIP! IT'S MUM!'

The boom-booming stopped.

'... No, I don't know what's wrong with the kiddo, Mum! Oh, I'm fine ... got a job in a pizza bar ...'

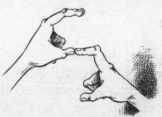

I don't want to listen to this! thought Bailey. How can Monty sound so calm? That's our mum on the phone! Our *mum*! And she *left* us! Why isn't he screaming and shouting and stamping his feet?

No, I'm not going to listen. I know! I'll start writing the first newsletter.

Bailey got a sheet of paper, a felt-tip pen and, sitting on his bed, began ...

Dear Scribblers,

    I want to tell you about something that has

Knock! Knock!
'W-what?'
Monty had opened the door.
'You want to speak to Mum, kiddo?'
'N-negative.'
'She wants to speak to you.'
'I'm b-busy.'
Monty closed the door.

changed my life. And I'm sure it'll

Knock! Knock!
'W-what?'
The Skipper opened the door.
'Your mother wants –'
'I'm busy.'
'But –'
'Negative!'
The door closed.

change yours too. It concerns a very special boy. His

Knock! Knock!
'Bailey-baby?'
'W-what?'
'Your mum –'
'Go away!'

name

'Knock! Knock!
'Sweetheart?'
'G-go away!'

was

Suddenly the door opened.

They were all standing in the doorway – the Skipper, Monty, Tiffany, Ma Glamrock.

Ma Glamrock was holding the phone. 'Your mum really wants to speak to you, Bailey-baby –'

'She does, Trooper Two.'

'Honestly, kiddo.'

'Have a chat, sweetheart!'

'Leave me alone!' cried Bailey. He jumped off the bed. 'I'm trying to w-w-work! I don't want to t-t-talk to anyone!'

He slammed the door in their faces.

Why should I speak to her? he thought angrily. She just left me. Without a word. Just a note –

Angrily he took the note from his pocket.

He tore it up, then threw it in the air.

For a moment the torn pieces fluttered around him like snow. Then . . .

A gust of air from the air shaft.

And –

Shweeeee!

The fragments of letter were sucked into the air shaft.

Good riddance! Mum's letter doesn't matter at all. All that matters is . . .

Scribbleboy!

THURSDAY

— 30 —

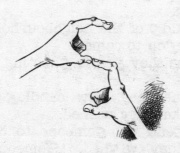

SCRIBBLENEW**S**
THE OFFICIAL NEW**S**LETTER OF THE
SCRIBBLEBOY FAN CLUB

I**SS**UE NUMBER 1

Dear **S**cribbler**S**

I want to tell you about **s**omething that ha**s** mega changed my life. And I'm **s**ure it'll mega change your**s** too. It concern**s** a very **s**pecial boy. Hi**s** name i**s** **S**cribbleboy!

Thi**s** i**s** the legend ...

Once the neighbourhood wa**s** nothing but concrete. Grey and flat and ultra-mega-boring.

The bird**s** tried to make thing**s** le**ss** boring by me**ss**ing on everything.

But that wasn't enough!

The earth tried to make things less boring by pushing weeds up through the concrete.

But that wasn't enough!

Some kids tried to make things less boring by writing graffiti.

But that didn't help!

Only one person could make the concrete less boring.

And the kids of the neighbourhood wished for that person to come.

Every time they saw a shooting star, they wished.

Every time they blew candles out on a birthday cake, they wished.

'Please send us someone to change the concrete,' they wished. 'Someone to give us dazzling colours instead of boring grey. We don't want to grow up like our parents and get used to the concrete!'

And one day, their wishes were answered.

Because, on a concrete wall, they saw

— 31 —

'Wait a minute!' said Ziggy.

'Wh-what's wrong, Zig?' asked Bailey. You've st-stopped reading the newsletter. D-don't you like it?'

'Like it!' gasped Ziggy. 'How can I *like* it? It's *wrong*!'

'H-how?'

'It's not the legend, Bay! Where did you get all this stuff about ... birds trying to make things less boring by messing on everything. And ... where is it? – Here! "The earth tried to make things less boring ..." Oh, it just goes on and on. And as for the kids wishing every time they saw a shooting star and birthday cake! Honestly, Bay! This is not the legend I told you. Oh, mind that kerb there!'

They were on their way to Pa Punkrock's so Ziggy could get a new mobile phone. Bailey was pushing the wheelchair so Ziggy could read.

'Affirmative, Zig! It's n-not the legend you t-told me! It's b-better!'

'*Better?* I'm sorry I brought the typewriter to the cinema for you to use if –'

'It's m-more interesting, Zig! There *is* a lot of b-birds' mess. And w-weeds. And gr-graffiti. If w-we use that in the legend it'll make it m-more –'

'*Better? Interesting?* Ain't they the words you used?'

'B-but, Zig –'

'And look here! At the end of the newsletter! You've signed it! Bailey Silk! Vice-President of the Scribbleboy Fan Club.'

'B-but I assumed I was!'

'You are! But where's my name? You haven't even thought to put a space where I can sign! And I'm the *President.*'

'B-but –'

'Oh, just leave me alone!' Ziggy shouted, shoving Bailey away from his chair. 'You want to take everything over!' He wheeled off on his own. 'You're trying to push me out of my own fan club! But I won't let you!'

'I'm sorry, Zig!' cried Bailey, chasing after him.

'Go away!'

'Please! Zig! I wasn't thinking!'

'You can say that again!'

'Zig! Stop! Please!'

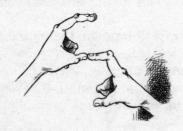

'You shouldn't have changed the legend without asking me!'

'I know, Zig! I know!'

'And you should have left room for me to sign!'

'I know! It's just that –'

'What?' snapped Ziggy, coming to a halt.

'Well, Ma Glamrock probably told you my mum phoned –'

'Oh, don't use that as an excuse!'

'I'm not ...! Look! I'll t-tear up the newsletter!'

'... What?'

'It's not worth us arguing! I'm going to tear –'

'No ... don't!'

'Don't?'

'No.' Ziggy calmed down, and slumped back in his

chair. He took a few deep breaths, then said, 'Perhaps
... well ... perhaps your version of the legend *is* a little
more interesting.'

'Do you think so, Zig?'

'... Possibly.'

'So you think we can k-keep it like this?'

'Affirmative.'

'So will you s-sign it, Zig? As President of the
Scribbleboy Fan Club?'

'Affirmative, fellow Scribbler.' Ziggy took the pen
and signed. 'There! And well done, fellow Scribbler. It's
a scribbledacious first *Scribblenews*.'

'Thank you, Zig.'

'Now ... let's get going. Otherwise we'll never get to
Pa Punkrock's. You keep pushing, Bay. It's quicker.'

'Affirmascribble.'

'What did you say?'

'Oh ... I'm not sure. My mind was miles away.'

'You said affirmascribble! That's great, Bay! I mean,
that's scribbledacious, Scribbler! That's what we'll say
instead of "yes" from now on: affirmascribble. And
"no" will be –'

'Negascribble!'

'Scribbledacious, Bay!'

'Mega-scribbledacious, Zig!'

'Ultra-mega-scribbledacious, Bay!'

'Totally-ultra-mega-scribbledacious, Zig!'

At that moment the Skipper strode round the corner.

'Morning, Trooper Two!' he declared.

He's not wearing his uniform! thought Bailey. At least, not all of it! Just the shorts, boots and shirt ... with the sleeves rolled up! The collar undone! And he's smiling! And relaxed. And holding his arm is –

'Hiya, babies!' said Ma Glamrock.

— **32** —

Bailey looked at Ziggy, speechless.

Ziggy looked at Bailey, speechless.

'You rushed out so early this morning, Trooper Two,' Skipper said. 'Didn't have a chance to tell you Ma Glamrock had agreed to come with me while I signed on today! And ... guess what?' He was beaming with joy. 'Mission successful!'

'What ... no nerve gas?' asked Bailey.

'Negative, Trooper Two.'

'No land-m-mines?'

'Negative, Troop –'

'Oh, do stop talking like that,' interrupted Ma Glamrock. 'Say "yes" and "no", like normal people.'

'He can say "negative" if he likes,' snapped Bailey.

Ma Glamrock looked at Bailey, 'Ooooo, you've got such a little temper, haven't you, Bailey-baby! Look at you! Your frown is deep enough to grow potatoes in! You need to lighten up! Ooooo, that reminds me!' She tugged at the Skipper's arm. 'Come on, Skipper-baby! You promised to have a good old boogie with me.'

'Affirm – I mean, yes, Ma Glamrock!'

And with that, the two of them rushed away, squealing 'ooooo' and 'eeeee' at the tops of their voices.

'Well, who would have thought it!' said Ziggy. 'My ma and your Skipper! Life is full of surprises, eh, fellow Scribbler?'

Everything keeps changing! thought Bailey. First Mum leaves. And I'm upset about that. Then I just about get used to living with the Skipper and Monty. And then – Monty meets Tiffany. And now ... oh, I'm not even going to think about it!

'Let's get to Pa Punkrock's so you can get your phone, Zig,' said Bailey, pushing the wheelchair. 'And, from now on, d-don't even *mention* anything to do with g-grown-ups. They do my head in!'

Pa Punkrock's shop was called Junk Iz Mee, and, from the outside at least, it certainly lived up to its name. The paintwork was peeling, the front door was hanging on by its hinges and the display window (which was cracked all over) revealed the goods on sale to be ... well, junk.

'Pa sells second-hand stuff mostly,' explained Ziggy.

'Looks more like twentieth-hand stuff,' commented Bailey, pushing Ziggy inside.

'Careful, Bay!' warned Ziggy. 'Don't touch the door. It might come crashing down on your head! And, careful! There's an old kettle on the floor ...' Then he called, 'PA!'

The shop looks even worse inside! thought Bailey. Just piles of old cracked records, radios with aerials missing, televisions with shattered screens, old paperback books, chairs with three legs, a table with no legs, and – Hang on! What's this?

'Zig! Look ! Is this w-what I think it is?'

'It's ... a photocopier, Bay!'

'This is just w-what we need, Zig!'

'Of course! To make copies of the newsletter, Bay!'

'Do you th-think your pa will let us have it, Zig?'

'I'll ask him, Bay! Where is he? PA! PA!'

'Let's ch-check if it works first, Zig. You plug it in there! That's it! Now, it's got some c-copying paper in already – good. Now ... let's see. I suppose you put w-what needs to be copied in here – you got the newsletter, Zig?'

'Here, Bay.'

'Thanks, Zig. Right! Now, I guess I close this ...' Bailey stared at the photocopier. '*Now* what do I do?'

'Press this, snotball!' said a voice.

A finger appeared and pressed a button.

The finger had a skull-shaped ring on it. The finger was attached to a tattooed hand. The tattooed hand was attached to a tattooed arm. Which was attached to a tattooed body – wearing a black ripped T-shirt (held together with safety pins) and the tightest leather trousers Bailey had ever seen. And on top of this body was a head with a huge blue Mohican haircut, ears jangling with earrings, and black make-up round the eyes.

'Pa!' cried Ziggy. 'Where were you hiding?'

'Not hiding, most beloved snotball,' replied Pa Punkrock. 'Out back, pondering a serious matter. You see, most beloved snotball, I'm going to change my hair colour!'

'Change the colour!' gasped Ziggy. 'But it's always been blue!'

'Not for much longer, most beloved snotball! A change is on the way! And as you know, hair colour is one of the most important things in a punk's life.'

'What's the new colour going to be?' asked Ziggy.

'Red, most beloved snotball! Though I'm not sure exactly what shade yet. Perhaps you can help.' He held three bottles of hair dye in the air. 'The choices are: Crushed Flamingo, Septic Toenail and Recently Punched Eyeball. What do you think?'

'Well . . . I'm not sure, Pa,' responded Ziggy. 'Perhaps you should ask Ma.'

'I will, beloved snotball. She's the one who'll have to dye it for me anyway. Now, how's that photocopy come out?'

'P-perfect,' Bailey told him.

'I'm over the moon, snotball!' declared Pa Punkrock. And spat.

Ting! went his spit as it hit a saucepan.

'Pa always spits when he's in a good mood,' explained Ziggy, smiling. 'Sometimes Ma Glamrock's mirrorball would be dribbling –'

'Don't talk about mirrorballs, most beloved snotball,' interrupted Pa Punkrock, shivering all over with disgust. 'Us punkrockers feel the same about mirrorballs as vampires feel about garlic.' He looked at Bailey. 'You must be the new best friend of my most beloved snotball. Snotty to meet you!'

'Er . . . snotty to meet you too,' said Bailey.

'Now, Ma phoned earlier and said you needed a new phone, most beloved snotball.' He took one from a cardboard box. 'Here we go.'

'Cheers, Pa,' said Ziggy, taking the phone. 'And one more thing –'

'What's that, most gleaming and cherished ball of snot?'

'Can we have the photocopier?'

'The photocopier? Why?'

'We just need it, that's all.'

'But it could fetch a good price, most beloved ball of snot! After all, it works! And not much in this dump actually does that.'

'Oh, *please*, Pa Punkrock!' pleaded Ziggy. '*Please!*'

'*Please!*' echoed Bailey.

'Well . . . let me think,' said Pa Punkrock, scratching

his head. Then, 'All right! You can have it! And do you know why?'

'Why?' asked Ziggy.

'Because seeing my most beloved ball of snot has made be feel snotty all over! In fact, I'm in the snottiest mood I've been in for ages. I'm as happy as a green glob of snot up a hairy nostril. I'm so snotty happy – I've got to pogo!'

Bailey looked at Ziggy. 'P-p-pogo?'

Ziggy said, 'If you thought Ma Glamrock's disco dancing was bad, wait till you see this!'

Pa Punkrock put a record on.

The record was scratched.

But it didn't matter! Because, as far as Bailey could tell, the record didn't have any melody. Or words! Just a monotonous yelling and a rhythm that went –

BAHM! BAHM! BAHM! BAHM!

'SNOTTY!' yelled Pa Punkrock, jumping up and down on the spot.

BAHM! BAHM! BAHM! BAHM!

Pa Punkrock jumped higher and higher.

And each time he jumped, he spat.

'SNOTTY!'

Jump!

Spit!

Ting!

'SNOTTY! SNOTTY!'
Jump! Jump!
Spit! Spit!
Ting! Ting!
Spit was flying everywhere now.
Bailey hid behind a gas cooker.
Ziggy hid behind a fridge.
'THIS IS THE WAY PUNKROCKERS DANCE!' shrieked
Ziggy above the roar of the music.
Pa Punkrock was jumping so high his head was
nearly hitting the ceiling.
'SNOTTY! SNOTTY! SNOTTY!'
Jump! Jump! Jump!
Spit! Spit! Spit!
Ting! Ting! Ting!

'WE'VE GOT TO G-GET OUT OF HERE, ZIG!' cried Bailey. 'LOOK! HERE'S SOME PHOTOCOPYING PAPER! IF I PUT THAT ON YOUR LAP – LIKE THIS – DO YOU TH-THINK YOU COULD B-BALANCE THE PHOTOCOPIER ACROSS YOUR WHEELCHAIR?'

'AFFIRMASCRIBBLE, BAY! IT'S NOT TOO HEAVY.'

'THEN LET'S GET GOING! AND WATCH OUT FOR THE SPIT!'

— 34 —

'Plug it in, Zig.'

'Affirmascribble, Bay.'

'Now, I'll just p-put it in here! Press this b-button! Don't stare at the f-flashing light, Zig! And then – the first copy! What do you th-think, Zig?'

'Scribbledacious, Bay!'

'Mega-scribbledacious, Zig!'

'Ultra-mega-scribbledacious, Bay!'

'Totally-ultra-mega-scribbledacious, Zig!'

'And I've just thought of another word, Zig. What we can call this place.'

'What, Bay?'

'Well, the Skipper calls home "HQ", so why don't we call this place "ScribbleHQ".'

'ScribbleHQ! That's a great idea, Bay. Scribblers meeting in ScribbleHQ and reading –'

'*Scribblenews*!' Bailey waved the newsletter in the air.

'Affirmascribble, Bay!'

BEEP! BEEP!

'Oh, pesky-pesky!' Ziggy took the phone from his pocket. 'Hello ... Yes, Ma! ... Well, obviously the new phone works ... I'm at ScribbleHQ ... Affirmascribble, that's what we're calling it now. And that's right, affirmascribble means yes ... All right, Ma, all right.' He put the phone back, then said, 'Ma says I've gotta go home for dinner, Bay. Shall we carry on with this in the morning?'

'Fourth copy! – Affirmascribble, Zig! Tomorrow will be f-fine! Besides, I want to try to d-design a badge tonight. Can I swing by your place and b-borrow your paints?'

'Affirmascribble, Bay. Scribblers should share everything.'

— 35 —

'What's this, Skipper?'

'Dinner, Trooper Two.'

'But it's not fishfingers and chips!'

'I thought I'd cook something different. Ma Glamrock gave me the recipe. It's called corned-beef hash.'

'Hash!' gasped Bailey, staring at the plate in front of him. 'It sounds like a disease to me!'

'Well, Trooper Two, if you don't eat that, you don't get any dessert.'

'Dessert!' cried Bailey, standing. 'But we don't have dessert!'

'Now we do, Trooper Two.'

'It's ice-cream, kiddo.'
'Don't tell me! Tiffany gave it to us.'
Monty and Skipper nodded.
'I'm going to m-my room!'

That's the right shade of red! And some yellow here ...
Scribbledacious! Now a few blue dots here – Ah! Not
quite the right blue. I'll add some white ...

Bailey was sitting cross-legged on his bedroom floor,
making the badges. In front of him were the paints,
some card (cut in badge-sized circles) and a small cup
of water to wash the brushes in.

He'd been working on the badges (one for him, one
for Ziggy) for nearly two hours. But to Bailey it seemed
like only two minutes.

Mmmm ... Now some circles here. Ah! Just right!
Exactly what Scribbleboy would have done.

Knock! Knock!

'It's me, sweetheart!'

Tiffany! Wonder how long she's been here?

'W-what?'

'I've just made some sandwiches for Skipper and
Monty. You want some?'

'Negascrib – I mean, negative! I'm too busy to eat!'

Made sandwiches! For my Skipper! The nerve!

Mmm ... a bit more yellow here, I think. Mega-
scribbledacious. Now, just make the 'S' a bit more
curved at the bottom –

Knock! Knock!

'Its me, kiddo!'

'I'm not hungry!'

'No, kiddo, it's not that. Me and Tiff have got
an announcement to make. Can you come out,
please.'

*

They were all in the living-room: the Skipper, Monty and Tiffany.

Monty was holding the largest bottle of champagne Bailey had ever seen.

'Now, I know this is all going to sound rather sudden,' began Monty, 'but . . . well, me and Tiff have thought about it. And – well . . . '

'What is it, Mont?' snapped Bailey. 'I'm b-busy.'

Tiffany started giggling. 'It's the peachiest-dandiest news ever!'

Bailey noticed her hair was beginning to spin.

'Tiffany and I . . . ' said Monty. 'Oh, *you* say it, Tiff!'

'WE'RE GETTING MARRIED!' announced Tiffany, giggling.

And now her hair was spinning full pelt.

The Skipper started clapping and cheering.

Monty popped the champagne.

It sprayed over everyone!

They all laughed!

Except –

'You're *what*?' cried Bailey.

'Getting married, kiddo!'

'But you've only known each other two seconds!'

'A bit longer than that,' corrected the Skipper.

'You *like* this idea, Skipper?'

'Affirmative, Trooper Two – I mean, yes, Bailey.'

'What? You're not calling me Trooper Two any more?'

'Ma Glamrock says you should call me Dad, too.'

'Ma Glamrock says!' cried Bailey, getting more exasperated by the second. 'Has the whole world gone crazy?'

'Now hang on, kiddo!'

'Calm down, Troop – I mean, Bailey.'

'What's wrong, sweetheart?'

'IT'S NOT SCRIBBLEDACIOUS BEING WITH YOU LOT!' he suddenly shouted, facing them. 'IN FACT, IT'S TOTALLY UNSCRIBBLEDACIOUS! AND IF YOU ASK ME IF THAT'S THE TRUTH, I'LL HAVE TO SAY "AFFIRMASCRIBBLE"! I WISH I COULD BE A SCRIBBLER LIVING IN SCRIBBLEHQ ALL THE TIME! BECAUSE DO I WANT TO LIVE HERE? NEGASCRIBBLE! ONLY BEING A SCRIBBLER IN SCRIBBLEHQ IS SCRIBBLEWONDERFUL! EVERYTHING ELSE IS TOTALLY-ULTRA-MEGA-UNSCRIBBLEDACIOUS!'

And with that, he went into his room and slammed the door.

— 36 —

Later.

Bailey was sitting on the floor in his bedroom, still painting the badges.

A bit more red here ... Affirmascribble! That's it! Oh, listen to them all! The Skipper, Monty, Tiffany. All laughing and joking. I bet Tiffany's hair hasn't stopped spinning all night. They've phoned Mum to tell her the news! Oh, well, I don't care. A bit more blue here ...

Later.

Tiffany's just gone. I heard her say 'I love you' to Monty. Then he said 'I love you' back. Now he's sitting in the kitchen talking to the Skipper. Who cares? I don't.

Some yellow dots here ...

*

Later.

They've both gone to bed now. I heard the Skipper say 'Goodnight, Troop – I mean, Monty', and then Monty say 'Goodnight, Skip – I mean, Dad'. Well, I'm not going to call the Skipper Dad. I'm fed up with things changing ... Red diamonds here ... And more circles, more circles ...

Later.

I'm the only one awake.

The badges are finished! Can't wait to show Ziggy in the morning. They're totally-ultra-mega-scribbledacious! Turn the light off ... Oh, it's a full moon tonight ... I wonder how Mum is?

A little later.

I should have spoken to her when she phoned! Wish I had! I want her to give me a hug! Oh, not the prickling in my eyes again! I can't bear it. One minute I don't care about anything. The next ... prickling.

A moment later.

I shouldn't have torn Mum's letter up! I want to read it again now. I'll get up on the bed ... Look into the air shaft ... There! The torn bits of letter ...! Can't get my fingers through the grille covering the air shaft ... What shall I do?

The very next moment.

I'm in the kitchen. Have to be quiet, though. Mustn't wake anyone. Tiptoe! Where is it? Monty only used it yesterday – Ah! Here it is! In the cutlery drawer!

The screwdriver!

*

Very next moment.

I'm standing on the bed. Unscrewing the grille in front of the air shaft. Got to get the pieces of letter back. Then I'll Sellotape them together ... Ah! Only one screw holding it on now! I can slide it away. Right ... let's reach out. Ahh ... can't quite reach the first bit of letter ...

Almost immediately.

I'm climbing into the air shaft. It's quite cold. Pipes running along each side. The pipes are gently vibrating and humming. Crawl along ... There! The first bit of letter! Now crawl a little bit further ... There! The second bit of letter ... And there's another bit ... Got it! And there's another bit down there! It's like a paper chase! Crawl ...

Look behind me!

There's the entrance to my bedroom. Mustn't lose sight of that. Don't want to get lost.

Where's the rest of the letter? There! Another bit ...

Crawl ...

Oh, I have to turn a corner now.

Got it ...! The next bit's even further ...

Hang on!

What's this? It's ... it's a diamond painted on one of the pipes. A bright red diamond with a blue heart inside it.

It can't be!

But it is!

'A Scribble!' gasped Bailey.

And there!
A blue star.
And there . . . further on!
A red heart.
Crawl forward.
A pink star inside a circle!
Crawl . . .
A yellow diamond!
This must be it! thought Bailey. Scribbleboy's
hideaway! Oh, look! There! Lots of tiny Scribbles all
over the pipes. It reminds me of something . . . What is
it? What . . . ?

I remember! A TV programme I saw once. About
explorers! Archaeologists I think they called them.
They went into ancient Egyptian pyramids. Saw writing

on the walls – hieroglyphics! That's it! Well, that's what this is like! But instead of pyramids, I'm exploring Scribbleboy's hideaway. And instead of hieroglyphics, there's –

Another Scribble!

And another!

More and more of them.

Crawl around this corner.

Still more Scribbles.

Up this little ladder.

The Scribbles are everywhere now! I can feel them whirling and swirling all round me. Reds, yellows, greens . . .

Crawl along here . . .

The tunnel's coming to an end.

I'm entering something bigger.

It looks like –

And then Bailey stopped in his tracks.

All he could do was stare.

At the most incredible sight he had ever seen . . .

— 38 —

Bailey was in a large chamber.

Like everywhere else in the air shaft, it was covered with pipes. Hundreds of them. Thousands. Across the walls, the ceiling; all weaving in and out of each other like spaghetti.

And over every pipe – and across the floor too – were Scribbles!

In fact, the whole chamber was one vast Scribble.

'Scribbledacious!' gasped Bailey.

And his voice echoed round him.

' . . . bledacious-dacious-cious-sssss . . .'

Bailey stepped forward.

I'm walking on a Scribble! he thought. Walking on comets and stars and moons. Oh, I'm feeling a little light-headed. Take a deep breath . . . That's better. Keep walking . . .

Look at that!

Cans of spray paint! Hundreds of them! Perhaps thousands! All lined up . . . reds, yellows, blues! The spray paint that Scribbleboy used! Look! There's actually a thumbprint on this one. A red thumbprint! Scribbleboy's!

Carefully Bailey put his thumb on top of the print.

The same size! My thumbprint matches Scribbleboy's exactly! Oh, this is just too totally-ultra-mega-scribbledacious.

Something on the ground!

What is it? Looks like a snake! All covered in green diamonds and yellow stars and –

Wait a minute! They're Scribble shapes and colours.

Closer . . .

It's a belt!

A belt covered in Scribbles!

And look here! Little loops of string all along the belt – Of *course*. Scribbleboy would put cans of spray paint in the loops! That's how he carried it all!

'Scribblebelt!' gasped Bailey.

And then Bailey saw something on the ground.

He picked it up.

A baseball cap.

It was covered with stars and comets and diamonds.

'Scribblecap!'

And then Bailey saw something else!
Something hanging on a wire coat-hanger.
Bailey stepped closer.
I don't believe it!
It can't be!
But it is –
And he tingled all over.
For it was a jacket!
A jacket covered in Scribbles.
'Scribblejacket!'

— 39 —

There were whirls and diamonds going down the left sleeve. Swirls and comets on the right. Stars on the collar. Hearts and circles on the back. And all kinds of wheeling and churning shapes and colours down the front.

It was the most beautiful thing Bailey had ever held.

This is *just* like that TV programme! he thought. An explorer finding the relics of a long-dead king! Only this is better! You can keep the treasure of Tutankha – oh, whatever his name is! This Scribblebelt, this

Scribblecap and this Scribblejacket mean more to me than all the jewel-encrusted masks and –

And then a thought –

Put on the belt!

Negascribble! I can't! This is the one and only Scribblebelt. I'm not worthy of wearing it! And yet –

Affirmascribble! I am worthy! No one worships Scribbleboy as much as me.

Slowly Bailey put on the belt.

It fits! Fits me perfectly! Feels so comfortable! This is just totally-ultra-mega-scribble –

And then another thought –

Put on the cap!

Negascribble! I can't! This is the one and only Scribblecap. I'm not worthy. And yet –

Affirmascribble! I am worthy!

Slowly Bailey put on the cap.

It fits!

And then –

The jacket!

Negascribble! That will be going too far. It's the one and only Scribblejacket. I'm not worthy –

And yet –

Affirmascribble! I am!

Slowly Bailey put on the jacket.

It fits! Fits me perfectly!

And that's when it happened!

His fingers started to tingle.

Then his hands . . .

His arms . . .

Chest . . .

His whole body . . .

And then he heard it!

A voice in his head –

Welcome back, Scribbleboy!

'Ahhhhh!' screamed Bailey.

And whipped off the jacket.

Instantly the tingling stopped.

And the voice.

Scribbleboy's power is in the jacket! thought Bailey.
And when I put it on –

He dropped the jacket!

Negascribble! I'm not ready for that! I'm not
Scribbleboy! I'm Bailey Silk! I can't do Scribbles! Not
like Scribbleboy! Tiny badges are my limit!

And yet . . .

That tingling felt so good. That voice so comforting.
'Welcome back, Scribbleboy,' it had said. Perhaps I am

meant to be Scribbleboy. The legend does say he'll return one day. Perhaps –

Slowly, he picked up the jacket.

Just touching it made his fingers tingle.

Blood pounded in his ears.

He put on the jacket!

Tingling! Whirling! Swirling!

Time to Scribble, Scribbleboy!

— 41 —

Affirmascribble!

You need some paints, Scribbleboy! Let's look at the spray cans! Oh, so many colours! Take a red – That's it! Exactly the right shade! And ... a few shades of yellow! A few greens! A black! That's it! Fill up every loop on your belt. Good, Scribbleboy! Good!

But how do I get on to the street? Don't say I've got to go back the way I came through the flat and –

Of course not!

Then how?

Think about it, Scribbleboy. If these are air shafts, there must be another way out. Down to the street. There're Scribbles to lead the way. Look! A diamond here! It leads down this ladder! Careful! That's it!

Now ... where?

There, Scribbleboy! A few stars. You see? They lead along this tunnel! Now down here!

I see now! Scribbles all the way! Down here! And down again! Ah! What's that light at the end of this tunnel? ... Let's crawl along ... There! I'm at ground level. This is the exit! There's a grating on here! I'll look through! Mmmm. The street beyond! Now, how am I going to get this grating off? I haven't got my screwdriver! Besides, the screws are on the other side –

Kick it!

Kick it?

It's the only way!

I suppose so ... well, here goes –

KA-BLANGGG!

The grating has gone! Now let's crawl out and –

Look how beautiful everything looks, Scribbleboy. The electric orange of the street lamps changes everything. Even the concrete is shimmering!

Affirmascribble!

Now where will you do your first Scribble?

Somewhere special!

But not too open! Don't forget! You mustn't be seen!

Affirmascribble! But it's got to be somewhere that will make other kids believe in Scribbleboy – Ah! Of course! I know *just* the place!

— **42** —

Run along here! What's that? A couple of people. Hide in the shadows here a moment! ... That's it! They're passing! Haven't seen me. Pull my cap down a bit lower though. Just in case.

There's the main road! Wait! More people passing. They sound drunk! Hide in the shadows ...

That's it. They've gone.

Just go down this street. Now down this alleyway.

And there – there it is!

That's what I'll scribble on.

A van, Scribbleboy?

It's not just *any* van! It's where Levi Toot hangs out. If I can get Levi believing in Scribbleboy, then the other kids in the neighbourhood will follow.

Good idea, Scribbleboy! What colour are you going to use first?

Red!

Go for it!

I'm spraying now! Look at it! So bright! Spray down the side of the van! Across here! Now a new colour –

Which one?

Yellow.

For the yellow moons?

Affirmascribble.

Go for it!

I'm spraying a yellow moon here! And now another here! And now ... Stars! Blue stars! Where's the spray can? – Here! Oh, how totally-ultra-mega-scribbledacious! Now, up on the roof!

A few comets here.

More circles ...

This is it! This is what I was meant to do! Nothing else matters –

'Yo!'

What's that? Someone's calling from the nearby flats.

'Yo! Up here!'

It's Levi Toot!

I didn't know he lived so close, but – there he is!

At his bedroom window!

In his T-shirt and boxer shorts!

And bleary eyed!

Wait!

His eyes are getting wider now!

Look at him!

His tongue's almost hanging out!

He can't believe what he's seeing!

'I know I'm a surprise!' said Bailey in his best rapping voice. 'But you gotta believe your eyes. So go and spread the word, 'bout what you seen and heard. Close your mouth before you dribble.' He jumped off the van, then ran into the shadows, calling, 'MY NAME IS SCRIBBLEBOY AND I'M BACK TO SCRIBBLE!'

FRIDAY

— 43 —

'Troop – I mean, Bailey?'

Bailey's eyes flickered open.

'Ziggy's on the phone for you.'

Bailey rubbed his eyes. 'Wh-what's the time, Skipper?'

'Nearly midday!'

'Midday!' gasped Bailey, sitting bolt upright. 'B-but why didn't you wake me up? What about the r-routine?'

'Ma Glamrock says the only routine I need is the beat of disco. And, after strutting my funky stuff a few times, I'm tempted to agree. Now, hurry up, Troop – I mean, Bailey. Ziggy's waiting!' The Skipper closed the bedroom door.

Bailey looked up at the air shaft.

The cover was screwed back on.

Last night seems so unreal now, he thought. Perhaps it was all a dream. After all, I don't remember coming back home. I don't remember taking off the Scribblebelt and the Scribblecap and the Scribblejacket . . .

He got out of bed.

Look at me! In my boxer shorts. The last person on earth who could be Scribbleboy. Ouch! What's that?

He'd trodden on something.

The screwdriver!

So *that* part wasn't a dream! he thought, clutching his hurt foot. So if I went to the kitchen to get that, then I -- Oh no! My hands!

They were covered in paint!

It's not a dream!

'Troop – I mean, Bailey,' called the Skipper. 'Don't forget the phone.'

The Skipper mustn't see my hands. I wish these boxers had some pockets in them . . . Now, creep out of the bedroom. Where's the Skipper? In the kitchen! Good. Now, back up towards the phone. That's it. Now . . . spin round! And . . .

'Zig?'

'Where are you, Bay? I've been at ScribbleHQ since ten o'clock. And I've written the second *Scribblenews*. Can't wait for you to read it!'

'Sorry, Zig. I-I don't understand. Why've you written another *Scribblenews*? We h-haven't given out the first one yet, Zig.'

'Oh . . . I forgot we were going to give them out!'

'F-forgot! But that's the whole p-point!'

'No problem, Bay. We'll give the first two out together. Now, how long you going to be, Bay?'

'Not long,' replied Bailey, thinking, I don't know – how long does it take to wash paint from your hands?

'Scribblebye, Scribbler,' said Ziggy.

'Scribblebye, fellow Scribbler.'

Bailey put the phone down.

'I'm just going out with Monty and Tiffany and Ma Glamrock, Troop – I mean, Bailey.'

'Out where?' asked Bailey, hiding his hands behind his back.

'Shopping. Tiffany wants to look at some wedding dresses. I've left you some chocolate doughnuts on the kitchen table for breakfast.'

'Ch-chocolate doughnuts!' gasped Bailey. 'What about our usual porridge?'

'Ma Glamrock says you have to have a chocolate doughnut in the morning. Otherwise the body's not prepared for strutting its funky stuff. And there's some money on top of the TV. Can you go to the video shop and pay for the damaged *Top Gun*? Say we're very sorry.'

'Affirmascribb – I mean, affirmative, Skipper. Bye.'

Shopping! Wedding dresses! Chocolate doughnuts! What's the world coming to? Well, I'll worry about that later! In the mean time – let's get my hands clean.

— 44 —

SCRIBBLENEWS
THE OFFICIAL NEWSLETTER OF THE
SCRIBBLEBOY FAN CLUB
ISSUE NUMBER 2

Scribbletations, Fellow Scribbers

Things are really zapping along in the
Scribbleboy Fan Club.

Bailey and me have started tidying up the
ScribbleHQ. We've cleaned most of the
auditorium. Next we're going to clean the
foyer –

'How do I look, Bay?' asked Ziggy. He'd just pinned
the badge Bailey had made to his anorak.

'Oh . . . what did you say, Zig? I'm trying to read the
Scribblenews you wrote.'

'Sorry, Bay! I just got carried away! The badge. How
does it look?'

'Scribbledacious, Zig.'

'Let me pin yours on – Where do you want it? On
your blazer?'

'Affirmascribble, Zig.'

'There! Totally-ultra-mega-scribbledacious, Bay. Now,
carry on reading! I won't interrupt again.'

After that we'll clean outside the
ScribbleHQ. Everything inside the corrugated-
iron fence will be – as Bailey says –
shipshape and Bristol fashion.

Bailey and me went to *S*ee Pa Punkrock ye*S*terday. And Pa Punkrock gave u*S* –

Bailey couldn't concentrate on the newsletter. His mind kept drifting off!

Where was Levi? He must have had a good look at his van by now! So why wasn't he here?

'Finished the *Scribblenews*, Bay?'

'Oh ... not yet, Z-Zig.'

'Well, hurry up! I want to start photocopying it.'

'Affirmascribble, Zig!'

– a photocopier.

*S*o Bailey and me have *S*tarted photocopying the *ScribblenewS*.

Bailey and me are going to give badge*S* to everyone a*S* well.

Bailey and me –

'Yo! Uniform Kid! Anorak Kid!' a voice cried.

It reverberated round the ScribbleHQ.

Bailey stopped reading.

Ziggy gasped out loud.

For at the back of the auditorium stood Levi.

'SCRIBBLEBOY IS BACK!' he announced.

'What?' gasped Ziggy.

'Wh-what?' gasped Bailey (acting as surprised as he could).

'Yo! He was on my van roof! And that's the truth – Yeeow!' Clap! 'Yo! Where are my homeboys?' He took a deep breath and called, 'HIP-HOP!'

Hip-Hop rushed in and stood beside Levi.

'What you all doing out there?' asked Levi.

'Yo! Chuck-a-boom!'

'Yo! You can all look at the old film poster another time.' Then he called, 'BE-BOP!'

And Be-Bop rushed in. 'Yo! Skoom-sha-skoom!'

'Yo! You've gotta stop moonwalking all the time, homeboy. You go backwards more than you go forwards these days.'

'Yo! Skoom-sha-skoom!'

'Yo! That's a good idea, homeboy. Walk backwards then you might go forwards more often.' Then Levi called, 'SHOO-WOP!'

And another boy rushed in.

He looked exactly like Hip-Hop and Be-Bop.

'This here –' said Levi to Bailey and Ziggy, pointing at the new boy, 'is the final member of my group. He's Hip-Hop's and Be-Bop's brother. They're identical triplets, as if you hadn't guessed. But – as with Hip-Hop and Be-Bop – there's a world of difference. Shoo-Wop here, you see, has bushier eyebrows. Say hello, Shoo-Wop.'

'Yo! Tisk-ta-tsk!' said Shoo-Wop, in the same drum-machine style as the others.

'Shoo-Wop can do the best back-flips I ever seen,'

said Levi. 'When Levi and the Homeboys gets going –
me rapping, Hip-Hop back-spinning and doing his
"Chuck-a-boom", Be-Bop moonwalking and doing his
"Skoom-sha-skoom", and Shoo-Wop here back-flipping
and doing is "Tisk-ta-tsk", we're the hottest, fastest,
loudest rapping group ever heard or seen in the
neighbourhood! And we're here to spread the word of
Scribbleboy. Ain't that right, homeboys?'

'Yo! Chuck-a-boom!'
'Yo! Skoom-sha-skoom!'
'Yo! Tisk-ta-tsk!'

'Y-you are,' gulped Bailey. While all the time he was
thinking, Levi believes in Scribbleboy! Look at him!
Smiling at me! Smiling at Ziggy! He wants to be part of
us. The same goes for Hip-Hop, Be-Bop and Shoo-Wop.
They're all giving me five. They want to give Ziggy five
too. But he's backing away and looking very uneasy –

'What's w-wrong, Zig?' asked Bailey.

'I don't understand this,' replied Ziggy faintly. He
looked at Levi. 'What do you mean, Scribbleboy's back?'

'Yo! I was in bed last night, when I heard a kinda
clunking. I know that sound! That's someone a-
stomping on my van! So I goes to my window. And
there he is! Scribbleboy! Scribbling!'

'Scribbleboy? Scribbling? On your van?'

'Way!'

'Negascribble,' said Ziggy. '*No way!*'

'Yo! Anorak Kid! Levi Toot don't lie! Come and see
for yourself!'

Bailey and Ziggy stared at the van.

Did I do that? thought Bailey. Must have done! But I don't remember doing half of it ... Oh, it's so beautiful. A true Scribble.

'What do you think, Zig?' asked Bailey.

Ziggy's mouth was agape.

'Close your mouth, Anorak Kid, before a fly gets in there. And that will give you a terrible scare – Yeeow!' Clap!

Hip-Hop was spinning on his back and going, 'Chuck-a-boom!'

Be-Bop was moonwalking and going, 'Skoom-sha-skoom!'

Shoo-Wop was doing his back-flip and going, 'Tisk-ta-tsk!'

Levi prowled round the van, rapping under his breath and going, 'Yeeow!'

They all look so happy! thought Bailey. Smiling faces everywhere. Except . . . Ziggy.

'What's wrong, Zig?'

But before Ziggy could reply, Levi strode up and put his arm around Bailey's shoulders.

'Wrong! What could be wrong? Ignore the Anorak Kid. He wouldn't know radical news if it jumped up and rapped in his ear! Yo! Scribbleboy's back! And we've got to spread the word, Uniform Kid. Tell every homeboy and every homegirl in the neighbourhood.'

'*Scribblenews*!' cried Bailey, getting caught up in Levi's enthusiasm. 'We'll do a new *Scribblenews* to report the sighting –'

'I've already done the new *Scribblenews*, Bay,' interrupted Ziggy.

'Yo! Whatever you wrote is history now, Anorak Kid! Ain't that so, Uniform Kid?'

'Affirmascribble, Levi!'

'Yo! We gonna get this fan club up and running. It's gonna be a mover and a shaker from now on. And it's gonna begin with a new – whatya call it – *Scribblenews*? And *I'm* gonna write it!'

SCRIBBLENEW**S**
THE OFFICIAL NEW**S**LETTER OF THE
SCRIBBLEBOY FAN CLUB
I**SS**UE NUMBER 3

Yo! Bro**S** –
All you bro**S**, li**S**ten up!
Thi**S** i**S** Levi Toot rapping.
That'**S** right – Me! Levi Toot!
The Main Man! The Big Chee**S**e!
The Numero Uno!
Or, rather, I wa**S**.
There'**S** a new Big Chee**S**e now.
And hi**S** name i**S S**cribbleboy!
That'**S** right!
Scribbleboy i**S** back!

Now, I know that **s**ome of u**S** bro**S** laughed when we heard thi**S S**tory before. But thi**S** i**S** me, Levi Toot, rapping – not that boy in an anorak or the other one in a **S**chool uniform – and I'm telling you that the legend i**S** true!

Co**S** I **S**aw **S**cribbleboy la**S**t night!

On my van!

And **S**cribbleboy told me to spread the word to all the kid**S** of the neighbourhood.

So, when you read thi**S**, you'd better take notice!

The **S**cribbleboy Fan Club meet**S** at the old cinema down the Big Road. Every day. At ten o'clock.

The Pre*S*ident i*S* Ziggy – that'*S* the bro in an anorak.

And the Vice-Pre*S*ident i*S* Bailey – that'*S* the bro in a *S*chool uniform.

But even though they wear the mo*S*t laughable clothe*S* in the neighbourhood – they are *S*till very cool homeboy*S*.

Yo!

Levi Toot

— **48** —

'It's scribblefabulous, Levi!' said Bailey, handing Levi back the newsletter. 'Not m-many rhymes though.'

'Easier to speak rhymes than write 'em, Uniform Kid. I'll start photocopying them – Yo! Hip-Hop! The back row needs to be dusted!'

'Yo! Chuck-a-boom!'

'Yo! Be-Bop! The floor could do with a sweep.'

'Yo! Skoom-sha-skoom!'

'Yo! Shoo-Wop! Polish the photocopier one more time before I use it!'

'Yo! Tisk-ta-tsk!'

The auditorium was nearly spotless now.

'What shall my homeboys start cleaning next, Uniform Kid?'

Ziggy came up and tugged at Bailey's sleeve.

'Not now, Zig! I'm s-sorting things out with Levi.'

'But, Bay –'

'Later, Zig,' snapped Bailey. Then walked off with Levi, saying, 'The foyer! That should be cleaned next.'

'What do you think, Uniform Kid?' Levi asked.

The foyer had been cleaned. There wasn't a shard of broken glass, or a speck of dust or rubbish anywhere.

Hip-Hop, Be-Bop and Shoo-Wop were standing proudly near by.

'Its scribblefabulous, Levi.'

'All these new words are so wicked! I'm going to learn every one! Yo! I've got an idea –'

'Bay!' Ziggy was tugging at Bailey's sleeve again.

'Not now, Zig! I'm busy with Levi.'

'But –'

'What's this n-new idea, Levi?' asked Bailey, walking off with him.

'A Scribbleboy dictionary! For all the new homeboys and homegirls who join the fan club!'

'Scribblefabulous idea, Levi! Now, can your homeboys clean outside –'

Bailey and Levi, followed by Hip-Hop, Be-Bop and Shoo-Wop, walked around the outside of ScribbleHQ.

Everything within the corrugated-iron fence was clean and tidy.

'You've done a scribblefabulous job,' said Bailey. 'W-well done, Scribblers.'

'Yo! Chuck-a-boom!'

'Yo! Skoom-sha-skoom!'

'Yo! Tisk-ta-tsk!'

'And now, my scribbledacious homeboys,' said Levi, handing them a pile of photocopied newsletters, 'we're going to go out and give one of these to every kid we see!' He looked at Bailey and smiled. 'Tomorrow, Uniform Kid, you'll have a ScribbleHQ full of Scribblers. And if that don't happen, I'll stop putting my cap on – Yeeow!' Clap! 'Gimme five, Uniform Kid.'

Bailey slapped Levi's hand. 'Scribblebye, Levi!'

'Yo! Uniform Kid!'

'Scribblebye, Hip-Hop!'

'Yo! Chuck-a-boom!'

'Scribblebye, Be-Bop!'

'Yo! Skoom-sha-skoom!'

'Scribblebye, Shoo-Wop!'

'Yo! Tisk-ta-tsk!'

And they left ScribbleHQ.

Alone, Bailey started thinking about Ziggy.

He rushed into the auditorium.

'ZIG!'

Empty.

Into the foyer.

'ZIG!'

Empty.

He must have gone home, Bailey thought.

Strange! Don't remember seeing him leave! I'll go round to see him before I go home –

At that moment he felt some money in his pocket.

Ah! That reminds me! The video store!

— **49** —

Bailey opened the door to Emporium Video.

Tring! went a bell above his head.

'A customer!' cried the owner of the shop, smiling very wide and rushing towards Bailey. 'My dear young sir, please browse! Browse to your heart's content in my empire of entertainment.'

The owner was in his late sixties and had a skull so smooth, it must have been shaven. He was wearing a red fez with a black tassel, a white tuxedo with silver rhinestones on the lapels, a black bow-tie, black trousers and black patent-leather shoes. Everything about him seemed polished and gleaming.

'Let me show you round, young sir,' he said, flicking on a small torch he was holding and shining it across the endless shelves of videos, just like an usherette shows you to your seat in a cinema. 'Now, here we have Action films. Explosions and that sort of thing. Don't like them myself! Last time I watched one I got so agitated I spilled my cocoa. Now, here are the Horror films – well, no point in even considering making cocoa if you intend to watch one of those! If you want to see horror, just look out of your window, that's what I say. And over here are the Comedies ... Then Science Fiction. Oh, here! Here are Family films. Oh, forgive the tears in my eyes, my dear kind young sir.' He took a handkerchief from his pocket and dabbed his eyes. 'Every time I think of family ... it reminds me of something very sad ...'

Bailey just stared, too fazed to speak.

'My daughter,' continued the shop owner. 'She left me, you see. Grew up and went to the other side of the world! I haven't seen her in ... oh, it must be nearly nine years now. So forgive my tears, my dear kind young sir.' He dabbed his eyes again. 'Let's depart from the Family video section, if you don't mind! I can't bear the distress any more, my kind young sir – Now, what video are you after? I can satisfy your every entertainment request. You name it, Butterfly Glitz will have it – oh, that's me by the way, Butterfly Glitz. Pleased to make your acquaintance, kind young sir.' He shook Bailey's hand.

Bailey was just about to say hello, but –

'Films are my life, you see, young sir!' cried Mr Glitz. 'I live for them! And this may only be a humble video store, but we must never forget we're dealing with movies! And all movies are big, it's just the screens that got small. Now –' He smiled wider than ever at Bailey. 'Name your video!'

'I . . . don't want a video!'

'You *don't*?' gasped Mr Glitz, still trying to smile. 'Then . . . why are you here?'

'Well, my brother already rented a video from you and –'

'Wait a minute, my kind young sir! Say no more! Is you brother's name Monty?'

Bailey nodded, amazed.

'And the film in question a certain *Top Gun*?'

Again a nod.

'Then you are Bailey, am I right?'

Nod.

'Then keep your money, my kind young sir. Keep it with my blessing. Put it back in your pocket and spend it on toffee. I know all about the unfortunate accident that happened to *Top Gun*. And the account is closed! And may I say what a pleasure it is to meet you at last.' And he started shaking Bailey's hand vigorously.

What's going on? wondered Bailey. Did Monty get here first and explain everything? He must have done. How else could he –

Tring!

'Hiya, Bailey-baby!' Ma Glamrock walked into the shop. She was holding a white, frilly dress, wrapped up in clear plastic. 'Fancy seeing you here!'

'Enter, enter!' cried Mr Glitz, shining the torch at Ma Glamrock. 'A more timely entrance could not be imagined.'

'I thought I'd just pop in and show you Tiffany's wedding dress,' said Ma Glamrock, holding the item up for inspection. 'It's frilly, but not too frilly. That's what they wanted. After all, it is only going to be a registry office do! But I think it's just groovy! I was thinking of sewing a few silver sequins round the neck and hemline. What do you think?'

Why's she asking me? thought Bailey. She must know I couldn't care less. And – more to the point – how did she know I was here?

'It's a humdinger,' replied Mr Glitz, shaking his head so that the tassel on his fez spun round and round. 'And I have some silver sequins that would be just right if you'd like them.'

Hang on! Ma Glamrock's not asking *me*! She's asking *him*!

'What has *he* got to do with it?' Bailey found himself asking out loud.

Ma Glamrock looked at Bailey. 'Why, don't you know who Mr Glitz is, Bailey-baby?'

Bailey shook his head.

Mr Glitz chuckled. 'No wonder you looked so surprised when I knew all about the video, my dear kind young sir. You see, Tiffany told me.'

'T-Tiffany!' gasped Bailey. 'But why?'

'Why shouldn't she?' said Mr Glitz, smiling his widest smile. 'After all, she *is* my granddaughter.'

I don't believe it! thought Bailey, rushing out of the shop. Tiffany's everywhere! I've got to speak to Zig! And quickly.

He ran all the way to Ziggy's house and knocked on the door.

'Who is it?' asked Ziggy from behind the door.

'Only me, Zig!'

'What do you want?'

'W-what do you mean? It's me! Your f-fellow Scribbler! Let me in!'

'No.'

'No? Surely you m-mean negascribble. Come on, Zig. Stop playing games. I want to talk to you.'

'I'm not playing games. And I don't want to talk to you! Go away.'

'But . . . why, Zig? What's wrong?'

'*You* know!'

'I don't, Zig! Honestly! Tell me! What have I done?'

Ziggy opened the front door. There was a cardboard box on his lap and he thrust it at Bailey. 'Take this,' he said firmly.

'W-what is it, Zig?'

'It's all the photographs of the Scribbles. I don't want them any more.'

'Zig! Tell me what's wrong! Please! As your fellow Scribbler –'

'I'm not your fellow anything! You have a new best friend now. Levi Toot! Go and talk to him if you want to talk. You've been talking to him all day. I'm sure he'll be interested in whatever you have to say.'

'Zig! Please! It's not like that –'

The door slammed shut.
'ZIG!'
Silence.
'ZIG!'
Silence.

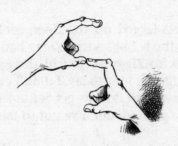

— 51 —

'What's this mess?' Bailey asked, looking at the plate in front of him.

'It's not mess, Troop – I mean, Bailey,' said the Skipper. 'It's called spaghetti carbonara.'

'It looks r-revolting.'

'It's not revolting at all, kiddo,' said Monty, forking some into his mouth. 'It's just not what we're used to, that's all. You have to try different things now and again. Remember that time I cooked ostrich?'

'That was revolting too!' Bailey pushed the plate away. 'I suppose it's another Ma Glamrock concoction.'

'Not at all, Troop – I mean, Bailey. It's Tiffany's!'

'That does it!' cried Bailey, standing. 'If I hear

Tiffany's name one m-more time, I'm going to explode!'

'Kiddo!'

'Troop – I mean, Bailey.'

Bailey stormed to his room.

Later.

Bailey sat cross-legged on the floor, looking at the photographs of the Scribbles that Ziggy had given him.

I want to talk to Ziggy so much! thought Bailey. I didn't mean to ignore him today. I didn't even realize I was. All I was trying to do was get ScribbleHQ clean. I thought he'd be pleased. Oh, I've got to talk to him –

Bailey dialled Ziggy's number.

Ma Glamrock picked up the phone.

'Hiya!'

'It's me! Bailey! Is Ziggy there, please, Ma Glamrock?'

'Oh, hiya, Bailey-baby. Well ... yes, Ziggy-baby is here. But he's already told me that if you phone he doesn't want to talk to you. Honestly! I've never known two boys argue so much! Now, I've got to go, Bailey-baby, because I've got to sew those sequins on Tiffany's wedding dress. She wants it as soon as possible. Seeya!'

'But –'

Click!

Later.

Bailey sat in his room.

Knock! Knock!

Monty put his head in.

'I've brought you an apple pie from work, kiddo.'

'I d-don't want it.'

'You must be hungry.'

'Go away!'

'I'll put it in the fridge for you.'
The door closed.

Later.

I wish there was some way I could make it up to Ziggy. The Scribbleboy Fan Club won't mean anything unless he's part of it! Oh, why didn't I talk to him more today? I should have done. Poor Ziggy! I didn't realize it was so easy to hurt people –

Knock! Knock!

'W-what?'

'Phone call for you, Troop – I mean, Bailey. It's Ziggy.'

Bailey grabbed the phone. 'Zig!'

'Good evening, Bailey.'

'Zig! I'm sorry! Really! I've been th-thinking about it. I was wrong. You're my b-best friend –'

'Why did Scribbleboy scribble on Levi's van?'

'W-what, Zig?'

'I know Levi might get other kids to join and all that. But it's *me* who's been a fan of Scribbleboy for longest. It's *me* who discovered Scribbleboy. So if Scribbleboy was going to return he should have revealed himself to someone special! And do a Scribble for someone special! Someone who deserves it! And that someone should be *me*! You understand what I'm saying? It should have been *me*! Don't you think so?'

'I . . . well, af-affirmascribble, Zig.'

'So I'm going to leave my wheelchair outside my flat tonight. It'll be tricky for me. It'll probably take me ages and ages. But I'll do it. And . . . well, perhaps Scribbleboy will come by. And – who knows? – perhaps he'll scribble on it for me.'

'P-perhaps he will, Zig.'

'And if he does, we can be friends again.'

Click.

Bailey stood there for a moment.

The dialling tone buzzed in his ear.

And he thought, Well, at least now I know what I've got to do.

— 52 —

Scribbletations, Scribbleboy!

Scribbletations!

Has everyone gone to bed?

Affirmascribble. I waited until I could hear Monty and the Skipper snoring before I unscrewed the grille. And I found my way here so much quicker. Hardly had to look at the Scribbles at all. And I've brought a bottle of turps and some rags with me this time.

Scribbledacious idea, Scribbleboy. Don't want to get caught with paint on your hands again.

Negascribble.

Does the jacket still feel scribbledacious?

Totally-ultra-mega-scribbledacious!

So, it's time to scribble – Wait! What's that strange gurgling noise?

Don't worry. It's just my stomach! I haven't had any dinner.

You shouldn't scribble on an empty stomach, Scribbleboy.

There's an apple pie in the fridge! I'll have it when I get back. But first . . .

Time to Scribble!

There's Ziggy's flat!

And there! He's put the wheelchair outside, just like he said he would.

Luckily it's very shadowy here. I shouldn't be seen.

Now, where shall I start?

The wheels!

I'll paint the spokes on the wheels!

Some red here ... Now some yellow ... Oh, that's mega-scribbledacious! These colours should all blur together when the wheelchair moves! Ziggy will love that!

Now down the sides ...

A comet here.

Now a moon ...

Some stars ...

Oh, ultra-mega-scribbledacious!

Now down the back.

A heart ...

Some circles ...

And that's it!

Finished –

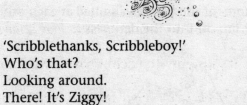

'Scribblethanks, Scribbleboy!'

Who's that?

Looking around.

There! It's Ziggy!

Watching me from his bedroom window!

And he's seen me!

Oh no, he's *seen* me!

'I knew you'd come, Scribbleboy! Because I'm your greatest fan! You know that, don't you, Scribbleboy?'

'Affirmascribble, Scribbler.'

'And I am the President of the fan club!'

'Affirmascribble, Scribbler.'

'And everyone has to do what a President says, don't they, Scribbler?'

'Affirmascribble, Scribbler.'

'Including Levi.'

'Affirmascribble, Scribbler.'

I've just realized! thought Bailey. I don't stutter when I'm Scribbleboy! This is totally-ultra-mega-scribbledacious!

Ziggy smiled. 'I'll always cherish my Scribblechair,' he said. 'And tomorrow, when I arrive at ScribbleHQ, everyone will see it. And they'll know how much you think of me. Won't they, Scribbleboy?'

'Affirmascribble, Scribbler.'

'Scribbletations, Scribbleboy,' said Ziggy, giving the salute.

'Scribbletations, Scribbler,' said Bailey, returning the salute.

And for a moment the two boys smiled at each other.

Then Bailey ran off into the darkness . . .

SATURDAY

— 55 —

'Morning, sweetheart!'

Bailey's eyes clicked open.

Tiffany was beside his bed, holding a cup of tea.

'W-what are *you* doing here?'

'I've brought you a cuppa, sweetheart,' she replied, putting it on the bedside cabinet, 'because there's no better way to start the day, and I always bring my sequinned sweetheart – oh, that's what I call my grandfather by the way – a cup of tea in the morning –'

'Wait!' cried Bailey. 'What I mean is – w-what are you doing here *now*?'

'Well, your brother and me were in your living-room making plans last night, and I got too tired to go home, so Monty made me a little bed on the sofa. Oh,

look! The cover to your air shaft has come a bit loose.'
She stepped forward to get a closer look.

'I l-like it that way!' said Bailey, jumping out of bed
to block her path. Then, suddenly realizing he was
wearing only his boxers, he grabbed a pillow and held
it in front of him.

Tiffany smiled. 'Oh, you mustn't be shy in front of
me, sweetheart. After all, we're practically family. Now,
drink your tea before it gets cold.'

A little while later.
  Knock! Knock!
  'Yo! Uniform Kid! You in there?'
  Bailey (dressed now) opened the front door.
  Levi strode in without being asked. 'Wanted to show
you this before the fan club met today,' he said,
indicating a sheet of paper. Then, 'Yo! Doughnuts!'
And he went straight into the kitchen. 'Doughnuts are
wicked.'

'Help yourself, sweetheart,' instructed Tiffany, who
had just put a plate of chocolate doughnuts on the
table, 'and would you like something to drink with
that? Let me see, you're a fizzy-orange person unless
my eyes deceive me, that right?'

'Yo!' nodded Levi, sitting at the table and tucking
into the largest doughnut he could find.

'Thought so, sweetheart, and luckily enough the
fridge is full of all types of fizziness – here were are!
Fizzy orange! And look at you! Second doughnut
already. Didn't you have any breakfast this morning?'

'No way! I was too busy writing this!' He tapped the
paper beside him.

'And what's that, sweetheart?'
'*The Scribbleboy Dictionary.*'
Red alert! thought Bailey. Levi talking to a grown-up

about Scribbleboy. And of all the grown-ups – Tiffany!

'And who might Scribbleboy be, sweetheart?'

'Yo! You know on the concrete wall in the old playground?'

'There's some very colourful graffiti there, yes, sweetheart.'

'Not graffiti. A Scribble! A Scribble by Scribbleboy –'

'Let's g-go!' interrupted Bailey, pulling Levi out of the room.

'Yo! But I'm still hungry!'

'Tough!'

— 56 —

THE SCRIBBLEBOY DICTIONARY

Scribbleboy	– The Main Man
A Scribble	– The Main Man's Stuff
Scribbler	– A Main Man fan
Scribblejacket	– The Main Man's jacket
Scribblebelt	– The Main Man's belt
Scribblecap	– The Main Man's cap
Scribbletations	– Yo! Hi!
Scribblebye	– Yo! Bye!
Scribblethanks	– Yo! Nice one!
AffirmaScribble	– Way
NegaScribble	– No way

Scribblespeak	–	The way Scribblers rap
Scribbledacious	–	Bad
Mega-scribbledacious	–	Very bad
Ultra-mega-scribbledacious	–	Even more bad
Totally-ultra-mega-scribbledacious	–	The Baddest
Scribblefabulous	–	Wicked
Mega-scribblefabulous	–	Very wicked
Ultra-mega-scribblefabulous	–	Even more wicked
Totally-ultra-mega-scribblefabulous	–	The Wickedest
Scribblewonderful	–	Radical
Mega-scribblewonderful	–	Very radical
Ultra-mega-scribblewonderful	–	Even more radical
Totally-ultra-mega-scribblewonderful	–	The Radicalest

What a strange dictionary! thought Bailey. It's not alphabetical, for one thing. And it's translated Scribblespeak into ... well, Levispeak. But I suppose it will help the kids around here to understand.

'It's totally-ultra-mega-scribbledacious, Levi!' Bailey told him, smiling.

They were walking down the concrete steps in Bailey's flats.

'Yo! Nice one, Uniform Kid – oh, I mean, Scribblethanks, Scribbler! Now I can give it to all the new homeboys and homegirls who'll join today. I hope there's enough photocopying paper. There's going to be hundreds of Scribblers. If not thousands.'

'D-do you really think so, Levi?'

'I *know* so. I was out late last night rapping till my jaws ached. Told every homeboy and homegirl I saw. Now, let's go to ScribbleHQ!'

'I've got to go r-round for Ziggy first,' said Bailey. 'I'll see you there later.'

There were outside the flats now.

'Yo! Way – I mean, affirmascribble! Gimme five!'

Slap!

And Levi ran off as fast as he could, yelling, 'YOOOOO! SCRIBBLEBOYYYYY!'

'Well, look at him go, sweetheart, looks like he's in a good mood.' Tiffany had come up beside Bailey. 'And this Scribbleboy certainly sounds like an interesting character.'

'There's no such th-thing as Scribbleboy.'

'*Really*, sweetheart?' said Tiffany, peering at Bailey. 'Then what's *that* all about?'

She pointed at something across the street.

And what Bailey saw made his mouth drop open.

For two kids were walking along, holding a banner.

And on the banner was written:

SCRIBBLEBOY FOR EVER!!

Levi's done it! thought Bailey. Look at those kids! They *believe*! The only thing is – Levi didn't tell them to keep it a secret!

'I've got to g-go,' said Bailey, striding away from Tiffany.

'Go where, sweetheart?'

'T-to Ziggy's.'

'What a coincidence, sweetheart, that's where I'm going, can't wait to see the sequins Ma Glamrock sewed on my wedding dress last night, so I can keep you company, ain't that nice, sweetheart?' And she started walking alongside Bailey. 'So, tell me about Scribbleboy.'

'I don't kn-know anything.'

'Well, those kids with the banner certainly seemed to know something . . .'

Why's she grilling me like this? wondered Bailey. She's driving me mad! I'm not going to answer any of her questions . . .

Walk a bit faster!

'So what's it all about, sweetheart?'

It's like the third degree, this is – Ahh! There's Ziggy's home!

Bailey rushed up and knocked on the door. 'Zig!' he called. 'Zig!'

Ma Glamrock opened the door.

'Hiya, Bailey-baby. Hiya, Tiff-baby! You're just in time – I was about to start strutting my funky stuff and I'd never have heard the door with all that going on. And I'm in dire need of a boogie this morning, I can tell you.'

'You do look a bit down in the dumps, sweetheart,' commented Tiffany. 'Do you think an Ice-Cream Diagnosis will help?' And she was already reaching for Ma Glamrock's pulse.

'Perhaps later, thank you, Tiff-baby. Why don't you come in and boogie with me for now. It'll help take my mind off things.'

'Off what exactly, sweetheart?'

'See for yourselves – Zig! Come here!'

Ziggy appeared in the doorway.

His wheelchair, of course, was covered in a Scribble.

Ziggy pushed past Ma Glamrock. 'Stop making such a fuss, Ma!'

'A fuss he calls it! I ask you! Look at it, Tiff-baby! He leaves it outside last night – without my knowledge, I hasten to add – and some joker does this! Ruins it!'

'It's not ruined, Ma. It's better than ever!'

Ziggy looked at Bailey and smiled.

Bailey smiled back.

There was so much the two boys wanted to talk about. But until they were away from the grown-ups, they had to contain their excitement.

'Better than ever!' gasped Ma Glamrock, glancing at Tiffany for moral support. 'You ever heard the like. Honestly, Ziggy-baby – this is taking it all too far.'

'Taking *what* too far, sweetheart?' asked Tiffany. Then, as quick as you like, added, 'You don't mean Scribbleboy, do you?'

'Oh, they've told you about that, have they?' sighed Ma Glamrock. 'Well, yes, Tiff-baby, that's exactly what

I mean. Ever since Ziggy-baby started this whole Scribbleboy thing –'

'She doesn't know anything!' snapped Bailey, glaring at Ma Glamrock.

Ma Glamrock noticed the intensity of Bailey's look and realized she'd made a mistake. 'Oh . . . I see . . . I'm sorry, Bailey-baby.'

'So Ziggy started it all, did you, sweetheart?' said Tiffany.

'I didn't start anything,' said Ziggy. Then shot Ma Glamrock a warning look. 'Did I, Ma?'

Ma Glamrock got the point. 'Why don't you come inside, Tiff-baby, and forget what I just said. I haven't got the sense of a lettuce leaf sometimes. And we've got more important things to worry about. Like disco dancing! And your wedding dress!'

Tiffany squealed with delight and rushed into the flat. 'Bye, sweethearts!' she called over her shoulder. 'And, for what it's worth, I think the wheelchair looks peachy-dandy.'

— 58 —

'That was close,' said Ziggy, sighing with relief. 'Let's get to ScribbleHQ. Push, Bay, will you? I'm a little tired today. I was up late last night waiting for Scribbleboy. And it was a lot of hard work to get my wheelchair outside – Wait! Bay! Look!' Ziggy pointed.

A group of kids were on the other side of the road. With the letter 'S' scrawled on their T-shirts.

'I saw a couple like that this morning, Zig. Only they had a banner! – Wait! Zig! Look!'

Now some more kids appeared.

These had the letter 'S' written on their baseball caps.

'Incrediscribble, Bay!'

'Mega-incrediscribble, Zig!'

'Ultra-mega-incrediscribble, Bay!'

'Totally-ultra-mega-incrediscribble, Zig!'

They turned the corner into the Big Road.

And saw . . .

Kids everywhere.

Kids with banners saying

SCRIBBLEBOY LIVES !

Or

WE LOVE SCRIBBLEBOY!

Or

SCRIBBLEBOY IS BACK!

Kids with 'S' on their T-shirts.

Kids with 'S' on their baseball caps.

Kids chanting, 'Scribbleboy! Scribbleboy!'

'There's hundreds of them, Bay!'

'If not thousands, Zig!'

And they were all heading for ScribbleHQ.

Bailey and Ziggy squeezed through the opening in the corrugated iron.

Kids everywhere.

Again, with 'S's on their T-shirts.

With 'S's on their baseball caps.

With banners saying, 'SCRIBBLEBOY' this, or 'SCRIBBLEBOY' that.

And all of them were talking about Scribbleboy.

The very air hissed with the 'S' of Scribbleboy.

'Scribbledacious, Zig!'

'Mega-scribbledacious, Bay!'

'Ultra-mega-scribbledacious, Zig!'

'Totally-ultra-mega-scribbledacious, Bay!'

'Let's get into the building, Zig! Can you manage, or shall I push?'

'I'll do it, Bay,' said Ziggy, easing himself forward. 'What's that everyone's reading, Bay? Did you write another *Scribblenews*?'

'Negascribble, Zig. It's *The Scribbleboy Dictionary*.'

'What a scribblefabulous idea, Bay. When did you do that?'

'It wasn't me, Zig.'

'Then who –?'

'Yo! I did it! Me! The one-time Main Man! The one-time Top Dog! The one-time Big Cheese! The one-time Numero Uno! Good to see you, Anorak Kid. You too, Uniform Kid. You're just in time. The meeting's just about to begin! Come into the auditorium! Out of the way, Scribblers. I want to push this wheelchair through –'

'I'll do it!' snapped Ziggy irritably.

'No trouble, Anorak Kid. Yo! Go through this FIRE EXIT door here ... aaannnddd – Yo! What do you think?'

The auditorium was full of kids. Circle seats as well as stalls. And more kids were flooding in all the time.

And across the ripped movie screen at the front was written:

Scribbleboy!

— 60 —

'What do you think, Anorak Kid?'

'That's Mr President to you, Scribbler!' said Ziggy firmly.

'Yo!' Levi jumped as if he'd been burnt. 'Listen to him, Uniform Kid –'

'And he's Mr *Vice*-President, Scribbler!' Ziggy said, just as firmly.

'Yo!'

Ziggy glared at Levi. 'Look at my wheelchair, Scribbler.'

Levi glanced down at the chair.

Then stared.

'Yo! It's ... it's ... it's ... ' He was too amazed to speak.

'Affirmascribble, Scribbler,' said Ziggy, nodding. 'Scribbleboy visited me last night. And you know what he told me?'

Levi shook his head.

'That I'm still the President. And everyone has to do what I say. Otherwise . . . I can *expel* them from the fan club.'

'Yo!' Levi gulped. 'The Main Man rapped all that to you?'

Ziggy nodded.

'But . . . I don't want to be expelled,' insisted Levi. 'That would be totally unwicked – I mean unscribblefabulous! Scribbleboy means a lot to me. And to my homeboys. We've written something. It's called the Scribbleboy Rap. We want to perform it to all the Scribblers here. If you expel us . . .'

'Oh, I won't expel you, Scribbler,' said Ziggy gently. 'What you've done in getting all these kids here is totally-ultra-mega-scribbledacious! You should feel proud of yourself. I know I'm proud of you.'

'You are, Anorak – I mean, Mr President?'

Ziggy nodded. 'Just don't forget who's in charge, that's all.' He held out his hand. 'Gimme five, Scribbler.'

Levi slapped his hand. 'Yo! Mr Prez!'

'And now,' continued Ziggy, 'it's time for me to welcome the new kids.'

'Scribbletations, Scribblers!' cried Ziggy, wheeling himself in front of the assembled kids. 'Welcome to the Scribbleboy Fan Club!'

The audience cheered wildly.

Ziggy motioned for silence and the crowd calmed.

'Once I had no friends,' said Ziggy. 'People looked at me and all they saw was an anorak. And an anorak in a wheelchair at that. So they didn't want to know me. At first it bothered me. I wanted to tell them, "I'm not just an anorak in a wheelchair. My name is Ziggy Fuzz and I'm interested in lots of things." But no one listened. And in the end it stopped bothering me. And I was all alone ... until I discovered Scribbleboy!'

Bailey and Levi were listening in the wings.

'The Anorak Kid is a wicked rapper,' said Levi, captivated by the speech. Then, noticing an angry glance from Bailey, quickly corrected himself. 'I mean, *Mr Prez* is a *scribblefabulous* rapper.'

'And then I realized, my fellow Scribblers,' Ziggy was saying, 'that I couldn't keep Scribbleboy to myself any longer. I had to share him with someone. So I wrote a letter to the one person who I thought would understand. Bailey Silk. And he *did* understand. And he became my first friend.' Ziggy looked at Bailey. 'Come out here and say hello, Bailey.'

Bailey hesitated, nervous.

'Go for it, Uniform – I mean, Mr Vice-Prez,' urged Levi, pushing him forward.

As Bailey stepped out the audience erupted with cheers and applause.

'This is your Vice-President,' Ziggy told them as Bailey stood beside him. 'And – in a way – it's because of him that we're all here today. Because Bailey taught me we had to keep telling more and more kids! We had to spread the word! And that's where Levi comes in – Levi! Come and say hello too!'

Levi stepped out beside Ziggy.

More cheers and applause.

Ziggy continued, 'You all know Levi! Him and his homeboys spread the word to all of you! And now we're all here. All Scribblers together. United by Scribbleboy!' And now his voice was reaching a crescendo. 'And we're going to keep the name of Scribbleboy alive! We're going to tell every kid we see. No kid should live without Scribbleboy! Spread the word!' Then he roared, 'SCRIBBLEBOY LIVES!'

And everyone roared back, 'SCRIBBLEBOY LIVES!'

And they all cheered and clapped until their throats were sore and their hands tingled.

'And now,' said Ziggy, as the noise subsided, 'Levi and the Homeboys – the most scribbledacious rapping band in the neighbourhood – are going to perform a special song called "The Scribbleboy Rap" for us. That so, Levi?'

'Way – I mean, affirmascribble, Mr Prez!'

'SCRIBBLERS,' announced Ziggy, 'I GIVE YOU LEVI AND THE HOMEBOYS!'

— 62 —

Hip-Hop started going, 'Chuck-a-boom!'

Be-Bop started going, 'Skoom-sha-skoom!'

Shoo-Wop started going, 'Tisk-ta-tsk!'

'Listen to that, Zig!' marvelled Bailey. 'It all blends together! What a scribbledacious sound! Look! My foot's tapping!'

'Affirmascribble, Bay! And look at all the kids! They're dancing along! Really enjoying it! This is so totally-ultra-mega-scribbledacious! And here comes Levi!'

Levi bounded in front of his three backing singers and rapped:

> 'Yo! Once this place
> was nothing but grey
> and all the grown-ups
> thought it had to be that way.
> But there was one kid
> and this kid knew the truth.

And one night he was seen
a-standing on a roof.

Scribbleboy! Scribbleboy!
Don't let the scribbling end!
Scribbleboy! Scribbleboy!
Come back and be our friend!'

'That last bit must be the chorus, Zig!'
'Affirmascribble, Bay. It's very catchy.'
'The audience are going wild.'
'Levi certainly is a scribblefabulous rapper.'
'Wait, Zig, Levi's off again –'

'This kid was wicked.
This kid was cool.
This kid was living
by a radical rule.
He said, "Go away, grey!
You don't belong here!
Cos everywhere I go
bright colours will appear."

Scribbleboy! Scribbleboy!
Don't let the scribbling end!
Scribbleboy! Scribbleboy!
Come back and be our friend!'

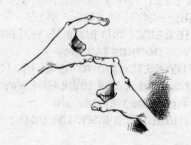

'I'm singing along with it now, Zig!'

'Me too, Bay.'

'And look – Hip-Hop's spinning on his back!'

'And Be-Bop's moonwalking!'

'And Shoo-Wop's back-flipping!'

'It's like one of those big stadium concerts I've seen on telly, Bay.'

'Affirmascribble, Zig – Wait! Levi's off again –'

> 'Yo! Scribbleboy was here
> and then he went away.
> Nobody knows where,
> but soon there'll be a day
> when he'll come back
> and save us from the grey.
> And all us kids
> are waiting for that day.
>
> Scribbleboy! Scribbleboy!
> Don't let the scribbling end!
> Scribbleboy! Scribbleboy!
> Come back and be our friend!'

And now everyone started singing along with the chorus:

> 'SCRIBBLEBOY! SCRIBBLEBOY!
> DON'T LET THE SCRIBBLING END!
> SCRIBBLEBOY! SCRIBBLEBOY!
> COME BACK AND BE OUR FRIEND!'

'THIS IS THE BEST DAY I'VE EVER HAD!' Bailey yelled over the singing. He grabbed Ziggy's hand and the two of them started to dance.

'AFFIRMASCRIBBLE, BAY! IT'S MY BEST DAY TOO!'

'SCRIBBLEBOY! SCRIBBLEBOY!
DON'T LET THE SCRIBBLING END!
SCRIBBLEBOY! SCRIBBLEBOY!
COME BACK AND BE OUR FRIEND!'

— 63 —

Much later.

Most of the kids had gone home.

Bailey and Ziggy left ScribbleHQ, exhausted and excited.

'No problems, Zig?'

'None, Bay.'

'I feel happy, Zig.'

'Me too, Bay.'

And Bailey said goodbye to Ziggy, still feeling problem-free and happy.

And he started walking towards his home, still feeling problem-free and happy.

And he went up the stone steps in his flats, still feeling problem-free and happy.

And he opened his front door, still feeling problem-free and happy.

And then he went into the living-room –

— 64 —

– and he had problems and wasn't happy.

'Sk-Skipper! Where's your moustache?'

'Ma Glamrock shaved it off, Troop – I mean, Bailey. I feel ten years younger. Funky, eh?'

'It's n-not funky at all. And wh-what are you wearing?'

'They're called flared jeans, Troop – I mean, Bailey. And this jumper is called a tank-top. Groovy, eh?'

'It's n-not groovy at all!' cried Bailey. 'Where's your hat with the feather? And your khaki shorts? And your –'

'Oh, I threw them all away, Troop – I mean, Bailey. Or rather, Ma Glamrock did. And then –'

'Don't tell me! Ma Glamrock bought you this ... outfit!'

'And it's not all on yet!' said the Skipper with a playful glint in his eye. He took something from a paper bag and hung it round his neck. 'A gold medallion!'

'You can't be s-serious!' cried Bailey.

'Well, it's not *real* gold! But it does the job.'

'*What* j-job exactly?'

'It turns me into a disco raver!'

I can't handle this! thought Bailey. I was happy a second ago. And then, as soon as I walk through the front door –

And, at that very moment, the front door opened and Ma Glamrock strolled in. 'Hiya, Bailey-baby! Hiya, Skipper-baby!'

— 65 —

'How did you get in?' asked Bailey.

'Your dad gave me a key.'

'A *key*? To *our* flat!'

'Wasn't that funky of him! And talking of funky, look at your dad! Doesn't he look the funkiest thing you've ever seen?'

'Only if f-funkiest means "total embarrassment"!'
snapped Bailey.

'Feel like strutting your funky stuff, Ma Glamrock?'
asked the Skipper, wiggling his hips.

'I'm always ready to shimmy and wiggle!' replied Ma
Glamrock, shaking her shoulders.

They're going to dance! thought Bailey with
mounting horror. I can't bear another moment of
this –

The front door opened again.

In walked Tiffany, holding a large plastic bag. 'Hello,
sweethearts!'

— 66 —

'But . . . h-how did *you* get in?' demanded Bailey.

'Monty gave me a key.'

'A *key*? To *our* flat!'

'Wasn't that peachy-dandy of him, well, I think it
was – Oh, Skipper! Look at you! You look so much
younger without your moustache. And those clothes! If
I wasn't engaged to Monty I might be tempted to tie
the knot with you – Tee hee! What a peachy-dandy
thing you are!' Then she looked at Bailey. 'Don't you
think so, sweetheart?'

'Only if peachy-dandy means "puke-making"!'

'Oh, I can see you're in another bad mood. But don't
worry, I've got something to cheer you up, my
wedding dress, it's in this bag, I've been ogling it ever
since Ma Glamrock gave it to me this morning.'

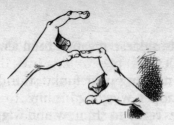

'Are you still pleased with it, Tiff-baby?'

'It's the peachiest-dandiest thing ever, Ma Glamrock, that's why I've brought it here for Monty to see – where is he? I thought he'd be home from work by now –'

The front door opened and closed.

'Evening all!' Monty strode into the room, carrying bags and bags of shopping.

He hugged and kissed Tiffany.

'Is that the dress, sweet thing?'

— 67 —

'It is, sweetheart!' Tiffany told him, holding it up. 'And what do you think?'

'It's whizzeroonie! Ain't it, kiddo?'

'Only if whizzeroonie means "most r-ridiculous thing I've ever seen"!'

'Oh, kiddo's in a bad mood!'

'That's what I said, sweetheart.'

'Bailey-baby needs to lighten up and strut his funky stuff.'

'Affirm – I mean, yes! Feel like a boogie, Troop – I mean, Bailey?'

This is a madhouse! Bailey thought. Everyone has

gone stark raving bonkers. Oh, I can't wait to get back to ScribbleHQ. I feel like running back there right now.

'He don't need a boogie!' said Monty. 'He needs a pizza! And that's what I'm going to cook tonight. Pizzas for everyone.' He pointed at the bags of shopping. 'That's what all this food's for. Because I've discovered I have a very special talent ... Shall I tell them, sweet thing?'

'Go ahead, sweetheart!'

'I,' declared Monty, smiling proudly, 'am a Doctor of Pizza!'

— 68 —

'You're w-*what*?' cried Bailey.

'A Doctor of Pizza, kiddo,' replied Monty. 'Just like Tiffany is a Doctor of Ice-cream. I can give you a Pizza Diagnosis and tell you what kind of pizza you like – I'll prove it! Give me your pulse, kiddo.'

Monty grabbed Bailey's wrist. 'Mmmm ... tuna!'

'Peachy-dandy, sweetheart!'

'Groovy, Monty-baby!'

'First class, Troop – I mean, Monty.'

Monty felt Bailey's forehead. 'Annnnnd ... yes! Kidney beans.'

'Peachy-dandy, sweetheart!'

'Groovy, Monty-baby!'

'First class, Troop – I mean, Monty.'

Monty said, 'Stick out your tongue, kiddo.'

'Negascribble!'

'Come on, kiddo! I can't complete the diagnosis without your tongue.'

'Negascribble!'

And the argument would have continued were it not for –

Knock! Knock!

'I'll get it!' snapped Bailey. 'Nice to know there's someone in the neighbourhood who hasn't got our key!'

He opened the front door.

'A most hearty and warm good evening to you, kind young sir,' enthused Butterfly Glitz, shining his torch in Bailey's eyes. 'May I enter your humble abode?'

'Why not?' said Bailey. 'Everyone else has!'

— 69 —

'Please take your seats, ladies and gentlemen,' said Mr Glitz, striding into the middle of the living-room and smiling very wide. 'I have a very special announcement to make.' Then he directed everyone with the beam of his torch. 'Tiffany, my superstar! Monty! You two, sit

on the sofa; that way you can hold hands like the back-row lovebirds you are. Ma Glamrock, you sit on that armchair there. And Skipper, perhaps you'll sit on the other armchair. That's lovely. Bailey, you'll have to sit on the floor, I'm afraid.'

Bailey, too stunned to resist, sat.

'My dear ladies and gentlemen, as we all know, my dear granddaughter, Tiffany, my superstar, is to marry this fine specimen of manhood, Monty. And, may I say, my eyes brim with joy at the prospect!' And to prove the point, he whipped the silk handkerchief from his tuxedo pocket and dabbed his eyes. 'Now, I have been racking my addled old brains to think of a suitable wedding gift to give them!'

'Oh, Grandad, you silly sequinned sweetheart, you shouldn't worry your old baldy-dandy head about that, should he, sweetheart?'

'Certainly not, sweet thing.'

'But I *want* to worry about it,' insisted Mr Glitz. 'I want to give you both something very special. And this afternoon, when I heard you and Monty talking, it hit me like a bolt from the blue!' The tassel on his fez started to spin.

'What, my sequinned sweetheart?'

'Well, my superstar, I heard you and Monty say how you wanted to own your own restaurant. A huge restaurant that cooked the best pizzas –'

'Yes!' cried Monty, getting very excited. 'Made by me, the Doctor of Pizzas!'

'– and made the best ice-cream –'

'Yes!' cried Tiffany, her hair beginning to spin. 'Made by me, the Doctor of Ice-Cream!'

'– and that's why,' continued Mr Glitz, his tassel spinning faster and faster, 'I'm going to give you the Pavilion.'

'The Pavilion!' cried Bailey. 'But ... that's what the old cinema is called!'

'That's right, my kind young sir,' said Mr Glitz, smiling the widest smile ever. 'Didn't you know? I used to run the Pavilion. Years ago! Oh, those were the days. When movies were big! But when times got hard, I had to close the place down. But I never sold it! It's still mine – Or rather it was! Because now it's my superstar's and Monty's to turn into a restaurant!'

'A restaurant!' Tiffany and Monty cried together, jumping up and down with joy. 'A restaurant! A restaurant! A restaurant!'

— 70 —

Bailey cried:
    'NNNNNNNNNNNEEEEEEEEEEGGGGGGG
GGGGAAAAAAAAAAASSSSSSSSSSSCCCCCCC
CCCCRRRRRRRRRRIIIIIIIIIIBBBBBBBBBBLL
LLLLLLLLEEEEEEEEEE!!!!!!!!!!'
    And ran to his room.

I won't let it happen! thought Bailey. ScribbleHQ turned into a restaurant!

Never! Never! Never!

I've been sitting in my room all night. Monty brought me some of the Pizza à la Bailey that he cooked. It tasted OK, I suppose. But I didn't enjoy it. How can I?

No more ScribbleHQ.

Negascribble!

I won't let it be!

But *what* can I do?

It's dark now.

Everyone's in bed.

Tiffany's asleep on the sofa. She and Monty stayed up until it was very late. Talking. Making plans. I heard Tiffany say, 'We'll call the restaurant SILK & SPANGLE.' What a ridiculous name!

Almost as ridiculous as her wedding dress! She asked her grandfather to take it back home and put it in her room –

Wait a minute!

The air shafts! They must connect all the flats! If that's so, then I must be able to get to Tiffany's flat.

And if I do that –
Affirmascribble!
I know what to do now!
Where's the screwdriver?
Here it is!
Right! Into the air shafts!
Tonight Scribbleboy will do such a Scribble . . .
A Scribble to make them all stop and think!

— 72 —

And Bailey was right.

For he was to do a very special Scribble that night.

A Scribble that would be remembered for a long, long time.

And the day on which it was found would always be known as –

SCRIBBLEDAY

— 73 —

Dawn over Scribbledom.

Slowly, the morning sunlight inched its way across concrete, weeds and graffiti.

It was the most dazzling sunlight Scribbledom had seen for ages.

Birds started singing . . .

And, one by one, the Scribbles became illuminated.

The intensity of the light made them shimmer and vibrate.

As if they were living things.

Living things waiting . . .

Waiting for Scribbleday to begin . . .

Mr Glitz woke slowly.

He'd been dreaming of a film premiere he'd organized at the Pavilion years ago. Oh, what a day that had been! There'd been crowds of people, film stars and, of course, journalists.

How the cameras had clicked and flashed when the rich and famous slid out of the black stretch limousines.

The Pavilion had looked so nice that evening.

He'd ordered potted palm trees for the foyer, and the kiosk was serving champagne and little sausages on sticks.

One of the happiest days of his life.

But soon there would be another happy day. Probably *the* happiest day: the wedding of his superstar, Tiffany, to that charming young man Monty Silk.

And Tiffany would look so glamorous in her wedding dress.

Just like a film star.

Mr Glitz got out of bed, put on a silk dressing-gown, then grabbed his torch from the bedside cupboard.

'Walk this way, please,' he said to himself, clicking the torch on. 'Just through here . . . That's right! Follow the beam of light! Now, into Tiffany's bedroom. I must take a look at all those shimmering sequins before I start the day.'

He opened the bedroom door.

The torch light beamed across the floor.

Then up . . .

Up to the wedding dress . . .

'AAAAAHHHHH!!!!!' screamed Mr Glitz.

The Skipper was easing himself out of bed very carefully.

He'd been strutting his funky stuff again last night and the muscles in his legs and stomach made him wince with pain.

Well, at least I've still got muscles in my stomach, he mused, heading for the kitchen. I thought they'd withered away years ago.

He took a pint of milk from the fridge and drank it straight from the carton.

And he was just about to grab a chocolate doughnut, when the phone rang.

Who can that be this early?

He picked up the receiver.

'Hello!'

'Mr Silk, good morning, my dear kind sir . . . I . . . I . . . '

'Morning, Mr Glitz. Is something wrong? You sound a little flustered.'

'Flustered, Mr Silk! Yes, dear sir, you could say that! I dropped my torch. It's broken! Smashed to smithereens!'

'Well, I'm sorry to hear that, Mr Glitz. But I'm sure you can get another one.'

'Oh, the torch is not important, Mr Silk. It's *why* I dropped it that matters!' He took a deep breath. 'Can I speak to my superstar, please. Something quite horrific has happened . . . '

Tiffany lay asleep on the sofa.

She was dreaming of all the new Spangle Specials she could make when she and Monty owned their new restaurant.

'Tiff!' The Skipper shook her awake. 'Tiff!'

'Oh ... er, morning, sweetheart,' she mumbled drowsily. 'What's wrong? Did I oversleep?'

'Nega – I mean, no, Tiff. It's still early. But your grandfather is on the phone for you. I think something's wrong.'

Tiffany dashed to the phone.

'My sequinned sweetheart! What is it? Are you peachy-dandy?'

'It's not me, my superstar,' explained Mr Glitz. 'But you should get round here as soon as possible.'

'But what *is* it, sweetheart?'

'It's your wedding dress!'

'My dress!' Tiffany put the phone down, then called, 'MONNNTYYY!!!'

— 77 —

Monty was asleep in bed, dreaming of all the Silk Specials he could make when he and Tiff opened their new restaurant –

'Mont, sweetheart!' Tiffany shook him awake. 'Mont!'

'Oh ... er, what is it, sweet thing? Did I oversleep or something?'

'It's not that, sweetheart, besides, you're not working today, if you remember correctly, but there's no time to lie in, sweetheart, my sequinned sweetheart just rang and ... something's happened to the wedding dress!'

— 78 —

Mr Glitz had just finished putting his clothes on when –

Knock! Knock!

'That'll be my superstar,' he said, rushing to open the front door.

'Oh, my sequinned sweetheart!' said Tiff, kissing him. 'I've brought Monty and the Skipper along.'

'Morning, Mr Glitz,' said Monty.

'Morning, Mr Glitz,' said the Skipper.

'A very good morning to you, one and all. Now please come this way.' Mr Glitz led the way to Tiffany's bedroom. 'I wish I could light your path with my torch, as is my custom, but, alas, as you probably all know ... the torch is no more. Now prepare yourself for a horrific moment!' He opened the bedroom door.

Everyone looked inside.

And gasped.

For the wedding dress had been spray-painted all over.

Emerald green! Ruby red! Sapphire blue!

And there were comets and stars and moons.

'But who ... who would do such a thing, sweet thing?' asked Monty, clutching Tiffany's hand.

'I'm not totally sure, sweetheart,' said Tiffany, 'but I saw something like this yesterday.'

'Where, sweet thing?'

'Where, my superstar?'

'Where, Tiff?'

Tiffany rushed to the phone. 'I need to speak to Ma Glamrock.'

— 79 —

Ma Glamrock was in bed dreaming of strutting her funky stuff with the Skipper.

BEEP! BEEP!

Still half asleep, she reached out to answer the phone.

'Mmmm –'

'Ma Glamrock! It's me! Tiff!'

'Tiff-baby! What's wrong? It's so early –'

'Ma Glamrock! Listen! Something's happened to the wedding dress!'

'The dress? Oh no – don't tell me, did the sequins fall off? I'm sure I sewed them on properly –'

'It's not the sequins, Ma Glamrock. They're still as firm as ever. Trouble is, you can't see them.'

'I . . . don't understand, Tiff-baby.'

'Someone got in my bedroom last night, I'm not sure how, but I have my suspicions, and they covered the dress in paint, Ma Glamrock, just like the paint I saw on Ziggy's wheelchair yesterday, and you seemed to know something about it all, sweetheart, and, oh, I don't want to put you on the spot, but *do* you know something? *Do* you? Please tell me! *Please!*'

There was a brief pause.

Then Ma Glamrock said, 'You best talk to my Ziggy-baby.'

— 80 —

Ziggy was dreaming of yesterday at ScribbleHQ. All those people, the rap, the laughter –

'Ziggy-baby?'

He struggled awake and blinked at Ma Glamrock. 'What is it, Ma? Bit early for you, ain't it?'

'Tiff-baby wants to talk to you,' said Ma Glamrock, handing him the phone, then rushing off to get dressed.

Ziggy took the phone. 'Hello?'

'Sweetheart,' said Tiffany, 'I'm not blaming anyone or pointing the finger, but someone has sprayed my wedding dress in the shapes and colours I saw on your wheelchair yesterday.'

Ziggy's heart missed a beat.

'A Scribble,' he said softly. 'On your wedding dress!'

'Sweetheart, you do know something about all this, don't you? Can you help us? Explain what's going on ...'

'I'm ... I'm not sure what's going on myself yet,' he replied. 'I need to speak to someone first.' He cut the call off, then dialled Bailey's number.

No answer.

He took a few deep breaths to calm down, then called Levi –

— 81 —

Levi was fast asleep, dreaming of rapping in front of a stadium full of fans, when he was woken by his mum, calling from downstairs –

'Levi! Levi!'

'Yo! What is it?'

'Someone called Ziggy's on the phone for you.'

'Tell him I'll see him later –'

'He said it's important, Levi!'

Grudgingly – Levi wasn't at his best first thing in the morning – he went downstairs and grabbed the phone. 'Yo! Prez!'

'Scribbletations, Scribbler!'

'Yo – sure! Scribbletations, Prez! I'm still half asleep. What is it, Prez, my man?'

'We've got a problem, Scribbler! I think our fellow Scribbler, Bailey, is in trouble. Meet me at ScribbleHQ as soon as possible. And bring Hip-Hop, Be-Bop and Shoo-Wop with you! We're going to need as much support as we can get.'

'Yo! Affirmascribble!' said Levi, suddenly wide awake.

— 82 —

Hip-Hop, Be-Bop and Shoo-Wop were asleep in one bed, dreaming of a world where everyone spoke in drum-machine language, when –

'Yo! Homeboys!'

Levi's voice calling them from the street outside.

They struggled, bleary-eyed, to the window.

'Yo! Homeboys! I know you're all tired, but get up and get fired – Yeeow!' Clap! 'Bailey is in a spot of bother! Get dressed and meet me at ScribbleHQ! Yo!'

'Yo! Chuck-a-boom!'

'Yo! Skoom-sha-skoom!'

'Yo! Tisk-ta-tsk!'

— 83 —

Ziggy was just leaving the flat, when Ma Glamrock rushed out with him.

'Where are you going, Ma?'

'To look at Tiffany's dress,' she replied. 'Bet I look a right mess as well. I haven't had time to put my make-up on properly! Or do my morning boogie!'

'You look scribbledacious, Ma!'

'Scribbledacious?' said Ma Glamrock thoughtfully. Then looked deep into her son's eyes. 'Ziggy, I can tell by your face you know more than you're saying. It's something to do with Scribbleboy, ain't it?'

'You mustn't tell them anything, Ma!' insisted Ziggy urgently. 'Scribbleboy is our secret! You promised! No matter how many questions they ask! *You mustn't say a word!*'

'All right, Ziggy-baby, all right,' said Ma Glamrock, trying to calm him. 'But it won't be easy.' She kissed him on both cheeks. 'You going to ScribbleHQ?'

'Affirmascribble! And don't forget, Ma! *Not a word!*'

'Not a word! Seeya, Ziggy-baby.'

'Bye, Ma.'

Levi was standing at the front of the auditorium, going over the words to 'The Scribbleboy Rap', when Hip-Hop, Be-Bop and Shoo-Wop walked in.

'Yo! Homeboys! The Prez ain't here yet. Don't let's waste time though! We should rehearse the dance routine for "The Scribbleboy Rap". Yo! Hip-Hop! Make sure you're not spinning on your back when we do the chorus! I've gotta hear your voice for "Scribbleboy! Scribbleboy!"'

'Chuck-a-boom!'

'Yo! Be-Bop! Make sure you don't get carried away with your moonwalking. Yesterday, you were out of the FIRE EXIT by the end of the song!'

'Yo! Skoom-sha-skoom!'

'Yo! Shoo-Wop! Make sure you've got enough space for your back-flips. You nearly landed on my head yesterday –'

'Yo! Tisk-ta-tsk!'

'Scribbletations, Scribblers!' cried Ziggy, entering the auditorium.

'Yo! Prez! What's going on? Me and my homeboys are a-wondering.'

'Sit down, Scribblers,' said Ziggy, 'and I'll tell you . . .'

Ma Glamrock found Mr Glitz's front door open. 'Only me!' she called, entering the flat.

'Ah, welcome, welcome, my dearest kindest Ma Glamrock,' said Mr Glitz, seeing her. 'Please enter! Enter my humble abode.'

'I came as soon as I could! Where's the dress?'

'Just follow me, my dear lady. As you see, I have no torch! Don't ask me what happened to it! I'm on the brink of tears as it is!' He showed Ma Glamrock into Tiffany's bedroom.

Ma Glamrock blew a kiss to the Skipper.

Smiled at Monty.

Said 'Hiya' to Tiffany.

Then she saw the dress.

'AAAAAHHHHH!' she screamed.

'Please, sweetheart,' said Tiffany. 'What can you tell us? I don't want to push you, but I have to know.'

— 86 —

Ziggy was telling Levi and the homeboys what he knew about Bailey and the scribbled-on wedding dress. Or 'Scribbledress', as it was now called. And, as each new phase of the story was revealed . . .

'Yo! Prez!' gasped Levi.

'Yo! Chuck-a-boom!' gasped Hip-Hop.

'Yo! Skoom-sha-skoom!' gasped Be-Bop.

'Yo! Tisk-ta-tsk!' gasped Shoo-Wop.

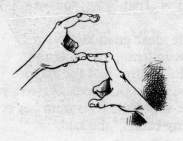

'Oh, Tiff-baby, I'd like to tell you,' said Ma Glamrock. 'May I never strut my funky stuff again if I'm lying, but ... but ...' Her bottom lip started to tremble with approaching tears.

'But what, Ma Glamrock?' asked Tiffany, gently squeezing her hand.

'I've promised my Ziggy-baby I wouldn't say a word. And I can't break my promise. Not to my very own baby.' She was weeping now. 'I ... just ... can't ...'

'Oh, sweetheart, don't upset yourself. We wouldn't ask you to break your promise, would we, sweethearts?'

'Nega – I mean, no,' said the Skipper.

'No, no, no, my dear lady!' said Mr Glitz.

'I s'pose not,' said Monty.

'So here's what we'll do, sweetheart.' Tiffany gave Ma Glamrock a comforting hug. 'Why don't we all go back to your flat and we'll ask Ziggy himself.'

'Oh, but you can't, Tiff-baby. Ziggy's gone to the – Oh, I can't tell you where! I'm sorry! It's part of the secret. I musn't say a word. Not a single, solitary word.'

Tiffany thought for a while.

'Then *don't* say a word, sweetheart,' said Tiffany, smiling. 'Just *go* there. Go to where Ziggy is. And we'll *follow*. In silence! That way, you won't break your promise!'

'Whizzeroonie idea!' cried Monty.

'Wonderful, wonderful, my superstar!'

'First class, Tiff! Really!' said the Skipper.

Tiffany looked at Ma Glamrock. 'Agreed, sweetheart?'

Ma Glamrock wiped the tears from her eyes.

'Follow me, my babies,' she said.

' . . . and that's all I know!' Ziggy finished.

'Yo! So our Vice-Prez, Bay – the Uniform Kid himself – scribbled on the dress.'

'Affirmascribble.'

'Yo! Chuck-a-boom!'

'Yo! Skoom-sha-skoom!'

'Yo! Tisk-ta-tsk!'

'But, Prez!' said Levi. 'If Bay is the one who scribbled on the dress, then that means –'

'What, Levi?'

'It means the Vice-Prez is . . . ' And Levi's eyes grew wide with wonder.

'Exactly, Levi,' said Ziggy nodding.

'*Radical!* – I mean, *Scribblewonderful!* Hey! What's that? A noise outside!'

Ma Glamrock opened the main doors to ScribbleHQ and entered the foyer.

She was followed by Tiffany.

Then Monty.

Then the Skipper.

And, finally, Mr Glitz, who was staring in amazement all round. 'It's much cleaner than I'd expected. That's where I used to stand to welcome the customers. Oh, I wish I had a torch. Feels strange being here without one – Wait! What's this on the floor?' He picked up a copy of *Scribblenews* (Issue Number 2, to be precise).

'And look!' said Monty, picking up another sheet of paper. 'This says *The Scribbleboy Dictionary*.'

'And the letter "S" written everywhere,' said the Skipper, looking all around. 'Ma Glamrock, do you know what's going on here?'

Ma Glamrock nodded, but kept her mouth shut.

'Don't keep asking poor Ma Glamrock questions, sweetheart,' said Tiffany. 'You know she can't break her promise – Wait! Did you hear that? Voices coming from the auditorium! Come on, sweethearts! This way ...'

— 90 —

'Voices!' cried Levi. 'Run! Run!'

'Negascribble, Scribbler!' declared Ziggy. 'We have a right to be here! This is ScribbleHQ. And we're Scribblers!'

'But –'

'No buts. I'm the President! We'll face whoever it is. Let me do all the talking. Agreed?'

Levi nodded.

So did Hip-Hop.

And Be-Bop.

And Shoo-Wop.

'Look!' said Ziggy, pointing. 'The door's opening.'

And in walked –

Tiffany.

Ma Glamrock.

Monty.

The Skipper.

Mr Glitz.

And all of them had wide eyes and open mouths.

They couldn't believe what they were seeing.

'Ma!' gasped Ziggy. 'You broke your promise!'

'I didn't, Ziggy-baby!'

'Then how – ?'

'Now, now, now, sweetheart,' soothed Tiffany. 'Don't go accusing your mum of anything. She hasn't said a word. Besides, we're only here to help. Ain't that right, sweethearts?'

'Of course, Tiff-baby.'

'You said it, sweet thing.'

'Affirm – I mean, yes.'

'A hundred times yes, my superstar.'

Levi shook his head sadly. 'This don't surprise me in the least, Prez. Mums and dads have strange ways, and it's us kids who have to pay – Yeeow!' Clap!

Tiffany, followed by the others, walked down the aisle and stood in front of Levi and his friends.

'Sweetheart,' she said, reaching for Ziggy's hand. 'You've got to tell us what's been going on. I have my suspicions, but I need to hear it from you.'

'Negascribble,' snapped Ziggy, snatching his hand

away. 'We'll never tell you anything. Right, Scribblers?'

'Yo! You said it, Prez!'

'Yo! Chuck-a-boom!'

'Yo! Skoom-sha-skoom!'

'Yo! Tisk-ta-tsk!'

Tiffany got to her knees, looked at Ziggy long and hard. 'I was hoping you would, sweetheart, because if I say who I suspect spray-painted on my wedding dress, I don't think certain people here are going to believe me. So are you going to help?'

'Negascribble!'

'Yo! You said it, Prez!'

'Yo! Chuck-a-boom!'

'Yo! Skoom-sha-skoom!'

'Yo! Tisk-ta-tsk!'

Tiffany stood up. 'In that case, sweethearts, we'd better go and ask Bailey what he was doing last night.'

'The kiddo, sweet thing? You can't be serious! He wouldn't know anything about this. Would he, Skip – I mean, Dad?'

'Negative, Troop – I mean, no, Monty! Never!'

'I knew you wouldn't believe me, sweethearts, and – who knows? – perhaps I am wrong! But there's only one way to find out . . . ' She started to walk out of the auditorium. 'To Bailey!' she cried.

'To the kiddo!'

'To Troop – I mean, Bailey!'

'To Bailey-baby!'

'To the dear kind young sir!'

Ziggy cried, 'Then we're coming with you! Right, Scribblers?'

'Yo! You said it, Prez!'

'Yo! Chuck-a-boom!'

'Yo! Skoom-sha-skoom!'

'Yo! Tisk-ta-tsk!'

Bailey's bedroom door opened.

And in came . . .

The Skipper.

Monty.

Ma Glamrock.

Mr Glitz.

Tiffany.

Ziggy.

Levi.

Hip-Hop.

Be-Bop.

Shoo-Wop.

And one at a time they said –

'Troop – I mean, Bailey's not here!'

'The kiddo's bed ain't been slept in.'

'So, where's Bailey-baby?'

'The kind young sir's bedroom is drafty.'

'It's coming from the air shaft, my sequinned sweetheart! Look! The cover's missing.'

'Scribbledacious, Scribblers!'

'Yo! You said it, Prez!'

'Yo! Chuck-a-boom!'

'Yo! Skoom-sha-skoom!'

'Yo! Tisk-ta-tsk!'

Tiffany picked up the screwdriver from the floor and looked at Ziggy. 'Bailey unscrewed it with this, sweetheart. And look! Scuff marks up the wall from him climbing inside! Why would he do all this, sweetheart? You've got to tell us! Bailey needs our help.'

'Oh, Ziggy-baby, *please* tell!'

'We all implore you, kind young sir.'

'Please, Zig. Kiddo needs us!'

'I'm so worried about my Troop – I mean, Bailey. Tell us what this is all about. *Please! Please! Please*, Ziggy!'

Ziggy thought for a while, then said, 'I need to talk to my fellow Scribblers first!'

— 93 —

Ziggy, Levi, Hip-Hop, Be-Bop and Shoo-Wop went out into the hallway.

Ziggy continued, 'I think you've all guessed what this means by now, fellow Scribblers: Bailey is Scribbleboy.'

'Yo! I knew it!'

'Yo! Chuck-a-boom!'

'Yo! Skoom-sha-skoom!'

'Yo! Tisk-ta-tsk!'

Ziggy said, 'So go out and spread the word. To every kid you see. Tell them Bailey is Scribbleboy. He did it to give us all hope. And now he needs our help. So go! Go!'

And, with that, Levi, Hip-Hop, Be-Bop and Shoo-Wop rushed out of the flat.

Ziggy wheeled back into Bailey's bedroom.

'I'll tell you what I know,' he told them.

Bailey lay curled asleep on the floor.

Gradually, voices filtered down the endless corridors of the air shafts and woke him.

He sat up.

That's Ziggy's voice! he thought. And Monty's! And the Skipper's! And . . . Tiffany's! Well, of course, it *would* be her! Sounds like they're all in my room! That means . . .

They've found the wedding dress!

And know *I* did it!

What shall I do?

Stay here! That's what I'll do!

I'm safe here in the Scribbleboy hideaway. Safe wearing the Scribblejacket. And Scribblecap. And Scribblebelt.

What's there to go back for?

To be told off for scribbling on the dress.

Oh, I shouldn't have done it. Not really. Me and my temper. Mum always said I'd do something I'd regret.

I've got no choice but to stay here.

For ever, if need be!

'. . . I suppose I always knew Bailey was Scribbleboy,' Ziggy was saying. 'That's why I was so upset when Levi's van got scribbled on. But . . . well, Bailey made up for it the next night. With my Scribblechair. And yesterday at ScribbleHQ was the most scribbledacious day we'd ever had.'

There was a breathless pause while everyone took this story in.

Then Mr Glitz said, 'Well, my kind young sir, all I can say is: one day that'll make a terrific movie.'

'The poor kiddo!' cried Monty. 'I'm so worried about him! He must be cold and hungry in there. He didn't eat any spaghetti last night, did he, Skip – I mean, Dad?'

'Not a morsel, Troop – I mean, Mont.'

'KIDDO!' called Monty, suddenly rushing to the air shaft. 'KIDDO!'

No answer.

'Let me try, Troop – I mean, Mont.' And the Skipper climbed up on to the bed and called into the air shaft, 'TROOP – I MEAN, BAILEY!'

Still nothing.

Then Ma Glamrock tried. 'BAILEY-BABY!'

Still nothing.

Mr Glitz tried. 'KIND YOUNG SIR!'

Nothing.

Tiffany. 'SWEETHEART!'

Nothing.

'The kiddo might be hurt!'

'Red alert! Red alert!'

'Oh, calm down, Mr Silk-baby.'

'Let Ziggy try calling. Will you do that, sweetheart?'

'Affirmascribble.'

Monty lifted him from the wheelchair and up to the air shaft.

'FELLOW SCRIBBLER!' yelled Ziggy as loud as he could. 'FELLOW –'

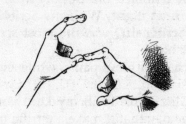

— 96 —

'– SCRIBBLER!'

That's Ziggy's voice!

But I'm not going back. They can call until their throats are sore.

I'm not going back –

'FELLOW SCRIBBLER!'

Here's the only place I feel safe. Here's the only place I can't be upset by the Skipper wearing flared trousers, or Tiffany being everywhere, or Monty calling the Skipper 'Dad', or Mum leaving altogether. Here's the only place I won't be told off for scribbling on the wedding dress.

'FELLOW SCRIBBLER!'

Bailey took a deep breath and yelled back, 'LEAVE M-ME –'

'– ALONE!'

'That's Bay!' gasped Ziggy.

'The kiddo!'

'Troop – I mean, Bailey.'

'The kind young sir.'

'Bailey-baby.'

'The sweetheart!'

Ziggy called again. 'COME OUT, FELLOW SCRIBBLER!'

'N-NEVER!' Bailey called back.

'Never!' shuddered Ziggy.

'Oh, the poor kiddo.'

'Poor Troop – I mean, Bailey.'

'Poor kind young sir.'

'Poor Bailey-baby.'

'Poor sweetheart.'

Ziggy said, 'We can't just leave him in there! He must be frightened. Oh, my poor fellow Scribbler –'

'Don't worry, Ziggy-baby. We won't leave him in there, will we, Mr Silk-baby?'

'Certainly not, Ma Glamrock. That's my Troop – I mean, Bailey, we're talking about. Right, Troop – I mean, Monty?'

'Right, Skip – I mean, Dad. And I know just what to do! I'm going in there after him.'

'But sweetheart –'

'I've got to, sweet thing! Can't leave my little brother all alone in the dark.'

'Troop – I mean, Monty's right, Tiff. Troop – I mean, Bailey's a stubborn thing. He might never come out of his own accord! So Troop – I mean, Monty has to go after him.'

'But my kind young sirs, the air shafts are like a labyrinth. They go on for miles and miles, all twisting and turning. It's like something from a science-fiction movie in there. Isn't that so, my superstar?'

'Very much so, my sequinned sweetheart. What if you go in and get lost, Monty my sweetheart? Then we'll have two of you to worry about.'

Ziggy declared, 'What a totally-ultra-mega-unscribbledacious mess.'

'The kiddo's friend is right.'

'I'm afraid so, Troop – I mean, Monty.'

'I'm afraid so too, my kind young sir.'

'Oh, my poor Bailey-baby.'

'The poor sweetheart.'

Then Ziggy said, 'I suppose there's only one person who knows *exactly* where Bailey is. Only one person who can climb into that air shaft, go straight to Bailey and get him out. And all without getting lost.'

'Who's that, friend of my kiddo?'

'Yes. Who, friend of my Troop – I mean, Bailey?'

'Who, my kind young sir?'

'Who, Ziggy-baby?'

'Who, sweetheart?'

'Scribbleboy!' announced Ziggy. 'The original Scribbleboy. Only *he* would know where the original hideaway is. Only *he* can help Bailey now.'

And that's when a voice said, 'I am that person!'

— 98 —

Bailey could hear something.

Not voices.

A scraping sound.

What's that? he thought. It sounds like – Affirmascribble! Somebody in the air shafts! And heading right this way! With hardly a hesitation. Somebody knows exactly where I am.

But that means . . .

Surely it *must* mean . . .

The only person who knows *exactly* where I am is . . .

The original Scribbleboy . . .

— 99 —

Levi was out in the street with Hip-Hop, Be-Bop and Shoo-Wop.

Levi stopped and told every kid they met ...

'Yo! Listen, Scribbler! You'll never guess who the new Scribbleboy is! Bailey! Yo! The Kid in the Uniform. We were as surprised as you! Ain't that so, homeboys?'

'Yo! Chuck-a-boom!'

'Yo! Skoom-sha-skoom!'

'Yo! Tisk-ta-tsk!'

'And now,' Levi went on, 'our Bailey needs our help. Spread the word. Tell every kid you see to meet outside Bailey's block of flats! – That's it! Run! Run! Come on, homeboys. Spread the word till every kid in the neighbourhood's heard – Yeeow!' Clap! 'Spread the word! Spread the word!'

— 100 —

Getting closer! thought Bailey.

Don't feel so safe here any more.

Tuck myself into the corner.

Closer ...

Can hear their breathing.

They're almost in the chamber.

Closer ...

They're crawling in ...

A hand ...
An arm ...
A shoulder ...
A chin ...
A mouth ...
A nose ...
The whole face!
  'YOU!' gasped Bailey out loud.

— 101 —

Outside, kids were congregating.
  Hundreds of them.
  Most with 'S's on their T-shirts.
  Or 'S's on their baseball caps.
  Or wearing bags with 'S' on.
  Some holding 'SCRIBBLEBOY FOR EVER' banners.
  Or 'WE LOVE S' banners.
  Or 'SCRIBBLEBOY LIVES' banners.
  All looking up at Bailey's flats.
  And talking about Bailey ...

Monty sat on Bailey's bed and buried his face in his hands. 'It's all my fault,' he sighed. 'I should have listened to the kiddo. I didn't realize he was this upset. Always teasing him about his frown.'

'Negative, Troop – I mean, no, Monty. It's me who's to blame. I should never have worn those flared trousers!'

'No, Mr Silk-baby! No, Monty-baby! I'm just as much to blame. I should never have made him strut his funky stuff.'

'Oh . . . no, my young kind sirs and madam. I'm sure I must be to blame somewhere. Perhaps I should have given him a funny cartoon video to watch. That would have cheered him up.'

Then Ziggy said, 'Shut up, you lot! I can hear faint voices coming down the air shaft. Bailey must be talking to . . . '

'B-but it *can't* be you!' declared Bailey, staring wide-eyed at the person sitting on the pipes opposite him. 'You of all people! I always imagined what the original Scribbleboy m-must have looked like. And he d-didn't look *anything* like you! It *couldn't* have b-been you! You *couldn't* have been Scribbleboy!'

'Oh, but I was, sweetheart,' said Tiffany. 'And surely you should start saying Scribble*girl*!'

— 104 —

'SCRIBBLEGIRL?' cried Bailey.

'Well, of course, sweetheart,' said Tiffany, smiling. 'After all, I *am* a girl, or hadn't you noticed? And be careful about your eyes, sweetheart, if they get any wider they might pop out of your head.' Tiffany looked round the Scribblechamber. 'Oh, it's years since I've been here, not since I was about your age, to be precise, sweetheart, glad to see that my painting is still looking peachy-dandy – Oh, look! There's my cluster of shooting stars on the ceiling! They were particularly difficult to do, had to stand on the pipes over there if I remember correctly. But they were worth it, don't you think, sweetheart?'

Bailey just stared, speechless.

'And look!' continued Tiffany. 'Over there! My bright

red comets, I used to have such fun doing those. I noticed a couple of peach-dandy comets on my wedding dress, sweetheart, so you must enjoy doing them too, am I right?'

Still Bailey just stared.

'And look! All those stars and diamonds down the pipes! How colourful they look! And, of course, my favourite shape is everywhere: the circle –'

'The c-circle!' gasped Bailey. 'Your f-favourite shape is the circle! I kn-knew it! I kn-knew it!'

'Well, I don't doubt you knew it, sweetheart,' said Tiffany, still smiling. 'Your Scribbles are every bit as good as mine, so you must understand me quite a lot.'

Bailey leaned closer to Tiffany. 'Tell me,' he said.

'Tell you what, sweetheart?'

'How it all st-started. How you b-became Scribbleboy – sorry, Scribblegirl!'

And for the first time since Tiffany had met Bailey, she became nervous and hesitant.

'Oh . . . I . . . I don't think I can, sweetheart.'

'*Please!*' urged Bailey.

'But . . . I've . . . n-never spoken about it before, sweetheart. N-not to anyone.'

'But I need to kn-know,' pleaded Bailey. 'And as a f-friend once said to me, it might help you to t-talk about things. Get them off your ch-chest.'

'Well, I'm s-sure it might, sweetheart. But . . . I don't know *how* to talk about all of that. Honestly I don't!'

'I've got it!' Bailey suddenly exclaimed. 'A way that m-makes it easier to talk. It worked for me, so it m-might work for you.'

'What, sweetheart?'

Bailey grabbed a can of paint and held it like a microphone. 'Tell me, Miss Spangle,' he said, 'have you ever w-watched *The Oprah Winfrey Show*?'

More and more kids were congregating outside.
Thousands now.
With 'S's on their T-shirts.
Or 'S's on their baseball caps.
Or wearing badges with 'S's on.
And they were beginning to chant.
Softly at first, but then growing louder:

> 'Scribbleboy!
> SCRIBBLEBOY!!
> SCRIBBLEBOY!!!
> SCRIBBLEBOY!!!!'

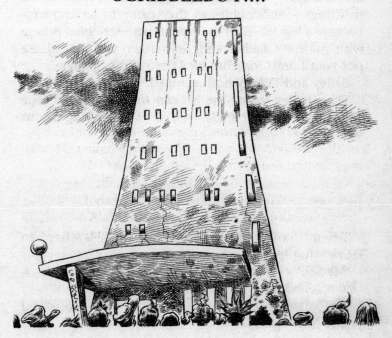

'Welcome, ladies and g-gentlemen,' said Bailey in his best chat-show-host voice, 'to the first edition of *The Bailey Silk Show*.' He giggled at the thought.

Tiffany giggled too. 'You sound peachy-dandy, sweetheart.'

'I learned it f-from Ziggy,' Bailey confessed, smiling. Then he took a deep breath and continued seriously, 'Today, ladies and g-gentlemen, we are going to discuss the story of one person. Many years ago –'

'Not *too* many years,' interrupted Tiffany.

'A *few* years ago,' Bailey corrected, 'this person painted on concrete walls and many other places. These paintings – or Scribbles as they came to be known – became a legend. And the person who scribbled is here with me now. Ladies and gentlemen, will you please put your hands together for Miss Tiffany Spangle.'

Bailey and Tiffany both clapped.

Then Bailey thrust the tin can under Tiffany's nose and said, 'Miss Spangle, tell us s-something about yourself.'

Tiffany took a deep breath. 'Oh, well, it's hard to know what to say, sweetheart –'

'Mr Silk!' corrected Bailey.

'Oh . . . what's that, sweetheart?'

'It's part of being in a ch-chat show. I'm Mr Silk and you're Miss Spangle.'

'Well ... Mr Silk, when I was a very, very young girl, younger than you are now, I lived with my mum and dad.'

'And were you happy, Miss Spangle?'

'Not really, sweet – I mean, Mr Silk. You see, my mum and dad were always leaving home.'

'Both of them?' gasped Bailey.

'That's right, sweet – I mean, Mr Silk. Not both at the same time, I hasten to add. One day I'd wake up and there'd be a note from Mum on the pillow beside me.'

'That's what my m-mum did!' gasped Bailey, forgetting his chat-show-host voice.

'Then you know what the letter said, sweet – I mean, Mr Silk.'

'Your mum n-needed time alone to think, Miss Spangle.' He remembered to use the correct voice this time.

Tiffany nodded. 'So Mum would be away for a few weeks. Then she'd come back and – guess what?'

'Your d-dad left, Miss Spangle?'

'He did, Mr Silk.'

'Another letter, Miss Spangle?'

'Another letter, Mr Silk. This time Dad needed time alone to think. So he'd stay away for a few weeks. Then he'd come back and – guess what?'

'Your m-mum would leave!'

'And so it went on, Mr Silk.'

'You must have had a lot of letters, Miss Spangle.'

'Hundreds! If not thousands!'

'So how did you c-cope with it all, Miss Spangle?' asked Bailey, leaning forward. Then he added, 'Wait a minute! I th-think I can guess! You went to live with your grandfather, Mr Glitz.'

'Exactly, Mr Silk.'

'And were you h-happy with him?'

'Oh, everything was just peachy-dandy. Except, of course, I brooded about my mum and dad. Because, you see, now I'd left home, they stopped leaving each other.'

'I see, Miss Spangle,' said Bailey, nodding thoughtfully. 'So you must have assumed they only left home because . . . ' His voice trailed away.

'They didn't want me, sweetheart,' said Tiffany, her voice breaking.

'Tiff,' said Bailey, 'you don't have to carry on if you don't want to –'

'But I do want to, Mr Silk,' retorted Tiffany as brightly as she could. 'It's very important you know.'

'Know what?'

'How the Scribbles started, of course.'

— 107 —

Tiffany took a deep breath. 'I'd always liked painting, you see,' she explained. 'And bright colours. Art was my favourite subject at school.'

'Mine too!' cried Bailey excitedly, forgetting his chat-show voice again.

'And, as I didn't have any friends –'

'Nor did I!' cried Bailey. 'At least, not until r-recently.'

Tiffany smiled. 'Well, you understand what I'm talking about, don't you, Mr Silk? What a peachy-dandy interviewer you are.'

Bailey remembered what he was supposed to be

doing. 'Thank you very much, Miss Spangle,' he said soberly. 'Now, let me g-guess what happened next – you painted things to take your mind off things.'

'That's right, Mr Silk. Just coloured-pencil shapes on sheets of notepaper at first. I could get lost in the patterns. I didn't think of Mum or Dad or anything like that. Just the peachy-dandy shapes and colours. But pretty soon, notepaper and coloured pencils weren't big enough or colourful enough! So I got bigger paper. Brighter paints. But pretty soon –'

'They weren't big enough or c-colourful enough.'

'Exactly! One day I got hold of a can of spray paint. I sprayed it on a wall. It looked –'

'Scribbledacious!'

'Just the word I was looking for, Mr Silk.'

'So tell us, Miss Spangle,' said Bailey, 'when did you discover this place?' He looked all around him. 'I'm sure our audience w-would really like to know that.'

'I discovered it quite early on, Mr Silk. You see, the air shaft cover in my room was missing –'

'It still is, Miss Spangle. That's how I got into your room last night.'

'I gathered that, Mr Silk. Anyway, one day I climbed into the air shaft – Oh, I knew it was silly of me. It could have been dangerous. And I'd like to warn all children who might be watching not to do such a stupid thing. But I needed somewhere to hide all my paints. There were hundreds of them by now.'

'How did you get so many, Miss Spangle?'

'I'm ashamed to say ... I stole them.'

'St-stole them!'

'From where my dad worked.'

'The garage! Your dad worked in the garage. That's why you scribbled on the chocolate machine.'

'I've always had a sweet tooth!'

'And the low concrete wall! The d-demolished house –'

'That's where my mum and dad lived, Mr Silk.' Tiffany sighed deeply. 'Oh, it was such fun doing the Scribbles. Climbing in here at night. Dressing up in my special outfit! Then dashing out and creating all my peachy-dandy shapes and colours! Oh, it was ... scribbledacious.'

'So why did you stop?'

Tiffany took a deep breath. 'I stopped, Mr Silk, when my mum and dad left me for good.'

'They *both* left? *Together?*'

'That's right, Mr Silk.'

'Where did they g-go, Miss Spangle?'

'To Australia!'

'What for?'

'To start an ostrich farm.'

'Ostrich! Monty cooked ostrich once.'

'He told me.'

'I couldn't eat mine.'

'He told me that too.'

'Has he told you everything?'

'Almost. Does that bother you?'

'I ... don't think so.'

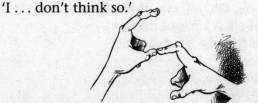

Tiffany smiled. 'I'm glad, sweetheart,' she said, reaching out for Bailey's hand. 'Because it shouldn't.'

'And ... so after your parents left, you st-stopped scribbling altogether?'

'Gradually, yes.'

'But ... why?'

'You know something, sweetheart, I've thought about this long and hard. And this is the conclusion I came to: my Scribbles were a way of letting my parents know I was ... well, in trouble, I suppose. Perhaps I secretly hoped that one day my mum and dad would see one of them and think, "Oh, our Tiffany needs us!

We'd best give her a hug and a kiss and stop leaving home." But they never did. And when they both left for good ... Well, I knew there was no point in scribbling any more ...' Tears sprang to her eyes and she started to cry.

Bailey got up and put his arm round her. 'But it *did* do good, Tiff,' he said. 'Because Ziggy saw the Scribbles. And he invented a legend. And that legend helped me.'

Tiffany nodded. 'You're right, sweetheart. It helped you make my favourite shape: the circle.'

'How do you m-mean?'

'Well ... in a way, that's what my Scribbles were trying to do, weren't they? To bring people together. And you've done that, sweetheart. Because of you, I met Monty. And the Skipper met Ma Glamrock. And Ziggy met me. Oh, the list goes on and on. And all because of you. Oh yes, sweetheart, you've created the best shape of all. A *circle* of friends.'

'A circle of friends!' gasped Bailey.

— **109** —

Outside, the kids were waving banners.

Levi was leading the chant of 'SCRIBBLEBOY! SCRIBBLEBOY!'

Hip-Hop was calling, 'Yo! Chuck-a-boom!'

Be-Bop was calling, 'Yo! Skoom-sha-skoom!'

Shoo-Wop was calling, 'Yo! Tisk-ta-tsk!'

And then, gradually, Levi started to change the chant to something else ...

'I'm sorry, Tiff.'

'What for, sweetheart?'

'For what I did to your wedding dress. And for being rude to you.'

'Forget it, sweetheart!' she said, smiling. 'We all do thoughtless things now and again! Sometimes without even knowing we've done them. Like when we upset you by announcing we were going to turn your ScribbleHQ into a restaurant!'

'I was *very* upset.'

'But we'll soon work something out, sweetheart. I promise you we will. And do you know why?'

'W-why?'

'Because we're a circle of friends. Now – come on! Let's get out of here.'

'Where you g-going, Tiff? This is the way out.'

'But this is my favourite way, sweetheart. Up that ladder. It goes all the way to the roof – Oh, by the way, I take it the interview is over now, Mr Silk?'

'Oh . . . I forgot! Affirmascribble, Miss Spangle, the interview is over.'

'So say "goodnight" to the audience, Mr Silk.'

'Scribblebye, audience.'

'Now – up that ladder!'

Ziggy said, 'They've stopped talking! Nothing's coming down the air shaft. That means Tiffany's taking him up to the roof like she said.'

'My sweet thing's taking the kiddo out!'

'Taking Troop – I mean, Bailey up!'

'Taking Bailey-baby up to the roof!'

'Oh, my superstar has done it! I'm so proud of her! Look at me! Getting all tearful again. Where's my handkerchief?'

Ziggy said, 'No time for tears! We've got to get up to the roof. Come on, you lot! We promised Tiffany we'd meet her up there. Let's go!'

'You're right! Let's go meet the kiddo and my sweet thing.'

'Meet Troop – I mean, Bailey and Tiff.'

'Meet Bailey-baby and Tiff-baby.'

'Meet the kind young sir and my superstar.'

And, just as they were all rushing out of the flat, Ziggy added, 'Meet Scribbleboy! And Scribblegirl!'

— 112 —

Levi had changed the chant now.

Everyone was performing the chorus from the rap, but with different words. Instead of Scribbleboy, they sang:

> 'BAILEY SILK! BAILEY SILK!
> DON'T LET THE SCRIBBLING END!
> BAILEY SILK! BAILEY SILK!
> COME BACK AND BE OUR FRIEND!'

— 113 —

'I'm getting t-tired,' panted Bailey, climbing up the ladder.

'Not far to go,' Tiffany encouraged from below him. 'Look up! Can you see that circle of light.'

'Affirmascribble!'

'That's the top! The roof!'

'But it looks so far away, Tiff.'

'No it's not, sweetheart. Keep climbing.'

Bailey went up a few more rungs.

Then stopped to catch his breath.

'You've got to keep moving, sweetheart!'

'But ... I'm ... breathless, Tiff.'

'Let me give you a little push, sweetheart. Does that help?'

'A little.'

'Then keep moving! That's it! Another step! One more! Now another! Another! Look, sweetheart! The circle is getting closer and closer!'

'I see it, Tiff.'

'Another step! That's it! One more!'

'We're nearly there now, Tiff! Just a few m-more steps . . .'

And then a hand appeared in the circle of light and reached down for Bailey.

It was a hand with a diamond ring on one of the fingers.

A hand he instantly recognized!

'Let me help you, cherub,' said a voice.

'Mum!' he gasped.

And grabbed hold of the hand –

— 114 —

– and was pulled up . . .

Into the arms of his mum.

She hugged him tight.

He hugged her tighter.

Everyone jostled round and embraced.

'You're safe, kiddo!'

'Safe, Troop – I mean, Bailey.'

'Safe, Bailey-baby.'

'Safe, my kind young sir.'

'Safe, fellow Scribbler!'

'Oh yes, the sweetheart's safe, and doesn't he look just peach-dandy in that jacket and cap?'

'He looks whizzeroonie, sweet thing.'

'He looks an officer and a gentleman, Tiff.'

'He looks groovy, Tiff-baby.'

'He looks like an Action film hero, my superstar.'

'He looks totally-ultra-mega-scribbledacious, Tiffany!'

Bailey looked at his mum. 'Do I look whizzeroonie and like an officer and a gentleman and groovy and like an Action f-film hero and totally-ultra-mega-scribbledacious?'

'Well, I'm not sure what half those things mean, cherub,' she admitted. 'All I know is ... you look different.'

'So d-do you, Mum.'

She was dressed more casually than Bailey had ever seen her: flowery silk skirt, denim jacket, T-shirt. And her hair was longer, hanging loose over her shoulders.

'Don't you like me this way, cherub?' she asked.

'It doesn't matter how you look. Who t-told you to come?'

'Why, your dad, of course. He phoned and told me you were in trouble. So I came straight away. Came straight to my cherub.'

'I wish you'd come sooner, Mum,' said Bailey. 'Everything kept changing. It was doing my head in.'

His mum hugged him again. 'I know, my cherub. I got so wrapped up in my own problems, I didn't realize how much I was upsetting you. But ... well, sometimes it happens. Grown-ups aren't perfect. We make mistakes. But I want you to know how sorry I am. So very, very sorry. And I want you to know this: no matter what changes in the future – and life is full of changes, believe me – one thing will always, *always* stay the same: I love you.' And she kissed him until his cheeks were very wet.

'Oh, where's my handkerchief?' cried Mr Glitz, wiping tears from his eyes. 'What a wonderful weepy this would make!'

'You're so right, Mr Glitz,' agreed the Skipper.

'You said it Skip – I mean, Dad.'

'Here's tissues for you all, sweethearts.'

'I haven't cried this much since my favourite lava-lamp exploded.'

'I've never cried!' said Ziggy. 'And I don't intend to start now!'

Then a new sound –

Panting!

And Pa Punkrock clambered on to the roof. 'I'm so out of breath I've swallowed all my snot,' he said.

'What are you doing here, Pa Punkrock?' asked Ma Glamrock.

'Looking for you, Ma Glamrock, that's what! Been looking all over the snotty place. So I followed the snotty crowds of kids and – here you are! On a snotty roof! It's not a disco party, is it? If it is, I'm getting out of here faster than a snotball from a sneezing nostril.'

'No, Pa Punkrock. It's not a disco party.'

'Snotty! Cos I need you to help me with a decision, Ma Glamrock.' He held the three bottles of hair dye in the air. 'What shade of red should my snotty hair be? Crushed Flamingo, Septic Toenail or Recently Punched Eyeball?'

'Oh, I don't care about your silly hair –' began Ma Glamrock.

'Recently Punched Eyeball!' interrupted Bailey.

'You . . . you sure, friend of my most beloved snotball?'

'Affirmascribble – I mean, yes.'

Pa Punkrock grinned very wide. 'You're right! Recently Punched Eyeball it is! Snotty! Snotty! Snotty! – What a clever snotball you are! No wonder the kids below are singing your snotty name!'

'Are they?' asked Bailey.

'They are, friend of my most beloved snotball.'

'They are, my dear young sir.'

'They are, sweetheart.'

'They are, Troop – I mean, Bailey.'

'They are, kiddo.'

'They are, Bailey-baby.'

'They are, fellow Scribbler.'

'They are, cherub.'

Bailey said, 'Let me see . . .'

— 115 —

Bailey walked to the edge of the roof.

Below were kids as far as the eye could see.

And in front of the crowd were Levi, Hip-Hop, Be-Bop and Shoo-Wop.

And all the kids were singing:

> 'BAILEY SILK! BAILEY SILK!
> DON'T LET THE SCRIBBLING END!
> BAILEY SILK! BAILEY SILK!
> COME BACK AND BE OUR FRIEND!'

The kids cheered when they saw Bailey.
Then continued singing:

> 'BAILEY SILK! BAILEY SILK!
> DON'T LET THE SCRIBBLING END!
> BAILEY SILK! BAILEY SILK!
> COME BACK AND BE OUR FRIEND!'

'You've got to say something to them, fellow Scribbler!'

'You must, Troop – I mean, Bailey!'

'Go for it, kiddo!'

'Say something groovy, Bailey-baby!'

'A heartfelt speech, my kind young sir!'

'Just spit on them, snotball!'

'Say whatever you like, sweetheart!'

'Speak loud and clear, cherub!'

And that's what Bailey did.

He shouted it as loud as he could, and without a stammer ...

'MY NAME IS BAILEY SILK AND I'M BACK TO BE YOUR FRIEND!!'

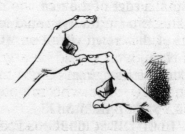

MONDAY
(ONE YEAR LATER)

— 116 —

SCRIBBLENEWS
THE OFFICIAL NEWSLETTER OF THE
SCRIBBLEBOY FAN CLUB
ISSUE NUMBER 107

ANNIVERSARY SPECIAL

Scribbletations, sweethearts

Who would believe it?

One whole year has passed since Scribbleday.

Doesn't time fly when you're having a totally-ultra-mega-peachy-dandy time?

So much has happened since the day I went into the air shaft to find our special sweetheart, Bailey. And – as it's the first anniversary of that day – I thought it would be a good idea to bring all Scribbleboy Fan Club members – especially the new ones who might not know the whole story – up to date.

Well, the first thing that happened after Scribbleday was ... well, me and Monty getting married.

Now I know it was only a registry office do, and in most people's eyes that's nothing to make a fuss about, but for me, my sweethearts, it was the most peachy-dandy day of my whole life.

Of course, I'll never forget the look on the sweetheart's face who married us. After all, we were quite a sight.

You see, Bailey had already scribbled on my wedding dress (that's another story, by the way, that any long-term Scribbler will tell), and we all liked it so much that we got him to scribble on Monty's white suit, and on my sequinned sweetheart's clothes, and on Mr Silk's and Bailey's mum's clothes, and on Ma Glamrock's and Pa Punkrock's clothes. And Ziggy, Levi, Hip-Hop, Be-Bop, Shoo-Wop – oh, everyone who was there was wearing Scribbleclothes. The photograph of us all standing on the Town Hall steps is one of my favourite things in the whole world.

Anyway, after the wedding, we had the problem of what to do with ScribbleHQ. We all talked about it lots and lots. Finally, it was Bailey's mum who came up with the answer: why don't we combine the fan club with a restaurant? And the rest – as they say – is history . . .

Monty and I transformed ScribbleHQ into a restaurant.

It took ten months.

Oh, what a lot of work it was. But everyone helped. And I don't just mean the workmen we hired to do the job. Oh no. Mr Silk swept up the rubbish, Levi and the Homeboys kept us entertained with songs (although there were times I felt that if I heard 'The Bailey Silk Rap' once more, I'd scream), Ma Glamrock kept up our spirits by dancing, Ziggy and Bailey's mum helped organize things, my sequinned sweetheart loaned us his new torch to see in dark places, and Pa Punkrock had great fun spitting at the workmen who fell asleep on the job.

And, of course, Bailey – my most special sweetheart – decorated every square centimetre of the place with his Scribbles (he's going to be a famous artist one day, I just know it!).

And when the restaurant opened we called it PLANET SCRIBBLEBOY!

And, I'm glad to say, it's been a peachy-dandy success.

And, more importantly, it's the meeting place for the Scribbleboy Fan Club.

We've got Scribbleboy memorabilia all over the restaurant: the Scribblejacket, Scribblecap and Scribblebelt are on view (protected in glass cases, of course), as are the original cans of spray paint, the very first issues of *Scribblenews*, the original *Scribbleboy Dictionary*, and all the clothes people wore at my wedding. Not to mention all the peachy-dandy photos of the Scribbles, taken by Ziggy.

Oh yes, my sweethearts, it's like our very own Scribbleboy museum.

Kids from all over the neighbourhood come in and talk (and, hopefully, eat one of my sweetheart's Silk Pizza Specials followed by one of my Spangle Ice-cream Specials), and it makes my hair spin and spin to see everyone having such a peachy-dandy time.

Finally, sweethearts, I'd just like to say a little thank-you to all those people who work at PLANET SCRIBBLEBOY: Mr Silk, our chief cleaner; Bailey's mum, our manager; Ma Glamrock, our top waitress (and, yes, sweethearts, I *have* warned her to stop wearing those platforms – I don't want her toppling over and spilling ice-cream or pizza into anyone's lap); and, of course, Pa Punkrock, our bouncer on Saturday nights, when things tend to get a little rowdy.

Also, a big thank-you to all our loyal

customers, in particular, Levi, Hip-Hop, Be-Bop and Shoo-Wop – whose rapping and dancing (those back-spins, moonwalking and back-flips are peachy-dandy) have kept us all so entertained.

And a very, very big thank-you to the one who, in a way, started it all: Ziggy.

It was Ziggy, as we all know, who created the Scribbleboy legend in the first place. (I understand he's working on a Scribbleboy book at the moment called *How To Be a Scribbler*, and I'm sure we all look forward to reading it when it's published – as I'm sure it will be.) Also, I'm sure Ziggy would like me to remind everyone that the fan club meets every Tuesday at 5.30 in PLANET SCRIBBLEBOY! Newcomers (or should I say new Scribblers?) are always welcome.

And, last but not least, a big thank-you to the one who brought us all together!

Bailey!

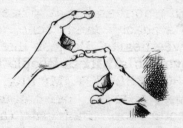

Sweetheart – and yes, Bailey, I'm talking directly to you now – Monty and I want you to know that when our baby is born (oh yes, that's my other piece of news by the way – I thought *Scribblenews* as good a place as any to announce it) ... anyway, when our baby is born, we want to call it Scribble Silk. (I think Scribble is a peachy-dandy first name for either a boy or a girl, don't you?)

So you see, my sweetheart, the circle just keeps on growing.

And now, as it's a special issue, all the founding members of PLANET SCRIBBLEBOY will sign off.

Scribblebye, sweetheart Scribblers!

Tiffany Silk

Doctor of Ice-cream at PLANET SCRIBBLEBOY

Monty Silk

Doctor of Pizza at PLANET SCRIBBLEBOY

Mr Silk

Chief Cleaner at PLANET SCRIBBLEBOY

Mrs Silk (known by all as Bailey's mum)

Manager at PLANET SCRIBBLEBOY

Ma Glamrock

Top Waitress at PLANET SCRIBBLEBOY

Pa Punkrock

Bouncer at PLANET SCRIBBLEBOY

Levi Toot

Best Rapping Customer at
PLANET SCRIBBLEBOY

Hip-Hop

Best Back-spinning Customer at
PLANET SCRIBBLEBOY

Be-Bop

Best Moonwalking Customer at
PLANET SCRIBBLEBOY

Shoo-Wop

Best Back-flipping Customer at
PLANET SCRIBBLEBOY

Mr Slitz

Most Sequinned Customer at
PLANET SCRIBBLEBOY

Ziggy Fuzz

President of the Scribbleboy Fan Club, now
based at PLANET SCRIBBLEBOY

Bailey Silk

Scribbleboy

PS The letter 'S' is mended at last!